THE MAN WHO WAS NOT

Gerald Dawson was the first to die — in an apparent road accident. But when members of his family receive telephone calls informing them of their own imminent demise, and the predictions come true, it's evidently the work of a serial killer. Police at Scotland Yard call in Sawley Garson, a specialist in scientific puzzles. Garson will need all his skills if he is to save the remaining Dawsons from the killer — a man who appears not to exist.

JOHN RUSSELL FEARN

THE MAN WHO WAS NOT

Complete and Unabridged

LINFORD
Leicester

Fearn, John Russell, *1908 – 1960*
The man who was not.—Large print ed.—
Linford mystery library
1. Serial murders—England—London—Fiction
2. Murder—Investigation—England—London—
Fiction 3. Detective and mystery stories
4. Large type books
I. Title
823.9'12 [F]

ISBN 1–84617–335–3

Published by
F. A. Thorpe (Publishing)
Anstey, Leicestershire

Set by Words & Graphics Ltd.
Anstey, Leicestershire
Printed and bound in Great Britain by
T. J. International Ltd., Padstow, Cornwall

This book is printed on acid-free paper

1

Gerald Dawson, twenty-six-year old son of Sir Robert Dawson, the eminent surgeon, had never done anything in his life to be particularly proud of. Bluntly, he was a waster, and far too much of a drinker. As the eldest child, he was distinctly a failure — a fact of which Sir Robert and his wife, Maude, were painfully aware.

This particular day in October represented something of a crisis in the life of Gerald Dawson. The gloom that obsessed him had something in common with the weather outside. His girl friend had at last realized the kind of fellow he really was and turned him down flat. Instead of an official engagement to one of the beauties of the younger social set, he found himself sitting in the lounge of the Cocktail Bar — his favorite retreat — with an unused diamond ring in his pocket and a positively foul temper clouding his mind.

With a drink in front of him he disinterestedly surveyed the softly lighted lounge. He recognized one or two habitués — and one or two strangers. Nothing unusual about that. The place was not a club anyhow: entirely open to the public, one of dozens of such places to be found in the heart of London. None of the newcomers was a woman, Gerald reflected, which was a pity. His one desire at the moment was to take up with another woman, if only to show his erstwhile girl friend that she did not count for much.

No — nobody interesting. Not even the quiet looking man in a nearby corner who had a peculiarly compelling face and almost colorless pale blue eyes.

Gerald grunted to himself, downed his drink, and then after due reflection left the Cocktail Bar and climbed back into his red sports car. He had just remembered Effie Brook: might be worth renewing acquaintance with her. She was blonde, very shapely, not too intelligent . . . Might be worthwhile. So Gerald weaved through the busy London traffic and towards eleven paid her a visit.

He emerged again with a metaphorical punch on the nose. Effie Brook was not so dumb as he had thought. So, disgusted with things in general, he returned to his sports car and spent the rest of the day in a useless round of old flames — to get the same answer each time. It was not to be wondered at that by the time he reached home — or more correctly the Georgian type residence owned by his father — he was not in a particularly good humor.

After having snapped off the heads of his two sisters he retired to his bedroom to start changing for dinner — when the extension telephone rang. Irritably he whipped the instrument up.

'Well?' he demanded, and the voice of the maid came to him from the hall.

'Somebody to speak to you, Mr. Gerald.'

With that she rang off and a more cheerful look came over Gerald's face. Probably one of the girls had changed her mind and —

'I have a message for you, Mr. Gerald

Dawson,' said a soft, mellow voice. 'I will make it as brief as possible. You will die at precisely nine o'clock tonight. Good bye.'

The line clicked. Gerald stared in front of him, at the telephone in his hand, then slowly put it back on its rest. Gradually his mind came back to normal.

'Dam' tomfool message,' he grunted. 'As if I haven't enough to worry over without that! Wait till I find who's responsible!'

He went on with his dressing, then paused in the midst of it and looked at himself, strange thoughts twisting in his mind. There was no doubt that he intended, originally, to dress for dinner — Then why on earth had he changed into a sports suit with its matching champagne-silk shirt. He pressed finger and thumb to his eyes and tried to recollect why he had done such a thing.

'But of course!' he exclaimed suddenly, recollecting. 'I'm going to see Betty! Wonder why it slipped my mind earlier?'

This was a question he could not answer. All that mattered now was that he visit her — and the fact that she lived fifty

4

miles away on the south coast did not alter his decision either. He reckoned he could cover the distance in his sports car in forty-five minutes.

In a far happier mood, even if there was some slight inward puzzlement, Gerald completed his dressing and then hurried downstairs. He nearly ran into June, his eldest sister, as he went across the hall. She looked at him in some surprise.

'Not staying for dinner?' she asked, rather dryly.

No.' Gerald pulled his overcoat and cap from the hall wardrobe. 'I've just remembered an important date.'

June smiled rather contemptuously. 'Correct me if I'm wrong, but would it be a woman?'

'Mind your own business!'

And with that chivalrous remark Gerald pulled open the main front door and slammed it behind him. In the space of a few moments he was on his way, his sports car roaring and snorting as it picked up speed down the driveway.

He noticed, though not for any particular reason, that it was five minutes before eight on the dashboard clock. Time for dinner at home. That was not the point. It meant that he ought to be at Betty's place by 8.45, if he went all out — and once free of the cramping London traffic that was precisely what he intended doing.

Muffled to the ears, his cap pulled well down against the cold of the dismal October night, Gerald cursed and accelerated his way through the city traffic, and succeeded in losing half an hour before he came to the clearer regions at the edge of the city. Then he really opened out, headlights blazing, and the speedometer needle gradually creeping up. At this rate it would be nearer half past nine when he reached Betty's.

Actually, when he came to ask himself the question, he did not know why he was so anxious to see her — or why he was going at such breakneck speed to do it. Still there it was, and he never let up his speed except when traffic regulation, or lights, compelled him to do so.

So, as he raced through the country roads under a black and starless sky, following the two tunnels of radiance made by his headlamps, he found himself thinking about that odd 'phone call he had received ... Death! At precisely nine o'clock! He scowled to himself as he tried to think who could have been responsible for such a rotten joke. He'd find out in time, and then there would be trouble.

Joke or otherwise, he could not help his attention straying ever and again to the dashboard clock, and as it began to near nine the thought crossed his mind that suppose it had not been a joke after all? Yet on the other hand, how could anybody possibly predict his death so accurately, especially when nobody knew where he was going, or what his intentions were?

'Ridiculous!' he exclaimed finally, and to prove just how he felt he jammed his foot down on the accelerator to floor level. Fast though it was traveling, the supercharged racer moved even faster. It leapt along the narrow hill-track road it was following — at the eastern end of the South Downs — and with a screech of tires swung towards the corner that loomed directly ahead.

Then something happened. Gerald had no idea what it was. Abruptly a blinding light, perhaps from an approaching car headlamp, swung straight into his face — a terrific effulgence which swamped him completely.

He simply could not see where he was going. The road had gone amidst the blazing brilliance — and a second later the road had gone altogether as the sports car jumped over its edge and went reeling and crashing into the waste land ten to fifteen feet below road level.

From light Gerald plunged into abysmal darkness. The night was split by the sound of cracking metal and shattering glass, then there dropped a complete quiet. The light that had virtually swept Gerald off the road had vanished — and somewhere in the ruins of the supercharged sports car a smashed dashboard clock registered one minute after nine.

★ ★ ★

By the usual avenues news of Gerald's accident finally reached home, and a long distance truck driver was responsible for the discovery. Instantly the police went to work to examine the scene, whilst Gerald's body was transferred to the nearest mortuary at Lessington, the nearest town to the scene of the accident. Then, inevitably, came the coroner's inquest.

The Dawson family was definitely shaken, though not greatly grieved, by the death of Gerald. He had always been a problem, anyhow. Quietly, each one told everything they knew, and there certainly was not a shred of evidence to suggest foul play.

The only one who slipped up, though not intentionally, was the maid — in that she never mentioned the 'phone call Gerald had received. In that she was not to blame, particularly as she did not know what the 'phone message had comprised.

So the business ended — for the time being, with the body buried and the Coroner giving a verdict of 'Death from Misadventure.' So perhaps the matter might have faded out completely had not November, a month later, seen a recurrence of the events which had led up to Gerald's death. And this time it was Trudy, the younger sister, who found herself involved — so much so she turned to Scotland Yard for help.

Her insistent pleas, and the fact that she was the daughter of the very eminent Sir Robert Dawson, finally gained her an audience with somebody who mattered — Chief-Inspector Hargraves, normally attached to the Homicide Division, but also an expert in various other branches of crime as well, particularly those of a baffling nature.

A tall, lean-faced, immobile man with thinning ginger hair, he sat looking at the dumpling of a girl across the desk as she agitatedly poured forth her story.

'It happened this afternoon at about half past three, inspector! A telephone call telling me that I'm going to die tonight at nine o'clock!'

Hargraves made a note and passed an unnoticed glance towards his right hand man, Sergeant Brice, who was unobtrusively shorthanding the interview from his own desk.

'Half past three,' Hargraves repeated, following some line of thought. 'And how was the call received, Miss Dawson?'

'How?' Her gray eyes looked indignant. 'I've just told you, inspector! By telephone!'

'Quite so, but was it on the direct line telephone, through an extension, or what?'

'Oh — er — the extension. There's one to every room in the house — every bedroom that is. There was a long pause when I said hello, and I began to think there wasn't anybody on the line — then just as I was about to put the 'phone down, a voice spoke. It didn't ask me if I was Trudy Dawson — it *said* I was, and then went on to say that I would die at nine tonight.'

'Can you give the exact words?' Hargraves asked.

'As near as I remember them he said 'I have a message for you, Miss Trudy Dawson. I will make it as brief as possible. You will die at precisely nine o'clock tonight. Good bye.' That was all. Didn't give me a chance to speak, or anything. I was so stunned I'd nothing to say, anyway.'

'I suppose,' Hargraves mused, 'the idea of a particularly cruel practical joker had occurred to you?'

'Yes, but . . . ' Trudy's plump face clouded. 'I can't quite credit that for two reasons. One is that I don't think anybody of my acquaintance would be so utterly beastly; and on the other hand my brother died in a road smash not quite a month ago — at nine o'clock at night. A coincidence, of course, but the time being the same I — I feel desperately uncomfortable.'

'That is understandable, Miss Dawson, but rather foolish. A connection between the two incidents is most unlikely. Come to think of it I remember reading about your brother's accident. Crashed in his sports car, I believe?'

'Yes — and on a perfectly empty road. That was the queer thing.'

Hargraves shrugged. 'That — without

wishing to sound callous — is beside the point, Miss Dawson. You have received this warning and in case it should be true you want police protection. You're quite entitled to ask for it, and we'll see that you have it. But first I'd like a few details.'

'Haven't I given them already?'

'I'd like to go further. A warning such as you have received, genuine or otherwise, is an indictable offence, and of course we want to trace the individual concerned. I gather it was a man. What kind of voice?'

'Very pleasant and deep. He sounded almost apologetic for warning me.'

'Thank you. Now, can you think of anybody who could really wish to have you out of the way? Don't pull your punches, Miss Dawson. Think hard, and be ruthless.'

There was a silence whilst Trudy went through all the manifestations of a mental struggle. Then at last she shook her head.

'Most people like me,' she said, rather naively. 'I'm quite certain there's nobody would wish to kill me — or play such a horrible joke upon me.'

13

'Which would seem to imply there is little need for alarm,' Hargraves smiled; and at that the girl's expression changed.

'Even so, I want protection!'

'You have my word. I'll contact the Divisional-Inspector for Kensington and have him arrange a detail of men.'

'But — why *him*? Aren't you going to do it personally?'

'It is not within my jurisdiction for me to do so. Your home is in Kensington, and it is the job of the Divisional-Inspector for Kensington to look after your interests. Everything will be attended to, and an effort will be made to trace the mystery caller. In that respect, unfortunately, we're handicapped.'

'How so?'

'Well, your 'phone is on the automatic dialing system, and most certainly the caller would also be on it. To trace a call on the dial system is impossible. There *are* ways, if desperate reason demands it, but so far that urgency has not arisen.'

Hargraves rose politely to signify the end of the interview, and Trudy too got to

14

her feet. At the door, as Hargraves grasped her extended hand, she looked at him seriously.

'Don't fail, inspector. I've got a sort of presentiment.'

'The guard will arrive about six o'clock,' Hargraves promised. 'The grounds of your home will also be under surveillance. You have nothing to fear. I would suggest you do not go far from home for the rest of the day.'

'I won't. I've only come out now in order to see you. As a matter of fact I was at a pretty hectic party last night and I've felt woozy ever since. Didn't wake up until noon. Anyway, inspector, thanks for all you're doing.'

'A pleasure, Miss Dawson.'

Hargraves closed the door upon her and then slowly returned into his office. Sergeant Brice glanced across at him.

'What do you make of her, sir? A spoiled miss with severe wind up?'

'Perhaps.' Hargraves looked at the notes he had made. 'Just perhaps, sergeant. I hope to heaven there's nothing in the girl's presentiment. Women are funny that way sometimes; they know a thing's going to happen before it does.'

There was a temporary silence as Hargraves' thoughts trailed off for a moment; then with sudden decision he picked up the telephone and started contacting the Divisional Inspector for Kensington.

* * *

Because the arrival of the men of the law would undoubtedly raise questions, Trudy lost no time when she returned home in telling her mother and sister the facts — and though they were mystified they agreed that the safest course was to call in the law. As it happened, Sir Robert Dawson came home from the hospital — where he was resident surgeon and consulting specialist — at the same time as the plainclothes men arrived. At six o'clock he alighted from his car to discover a squad car and four powerful men just behind him.

Sir Robert was nothing if not to the point. In the hall he cross-examined

16

Trudy as relentlessly as a prosecuting counsel — so much so he nearly had the girl in tears by the time he finished.

'All right, it's done now!' he said flatly, tugging off his hat and coat. 'But I don't think you need have been so precipitate in your actions, Trudy! Scotland Yard indeed — and all over a silly 'phone call hoax.'

'I did what I thought was safest, dad,' Trudy insisted.

'And probably wisest,' commented one of the p.c. men. 'Some criminals will get up to anything, Sir Robert — especially when the people concerned are connected with a famous man. Yourself, of course.'

Sir Robert sighed. He was a medium sized man with graying hair, horn-rimmed glasses, and an almost incredibly determined chin.

'It starts a lot of nasty publicity, that's all,' he said irritably. 'You don't suppose the fact that you men are here will escape unnoticed, do you? Not on your life! Detached though this house is there are still neighbors — damned unpleasant ones, some of them. They're going to enjoy the fact that a squad car has turned up at my home . . . If you ask me, the whole business is a lot of nonsense!'

Having thus made plain his reactions Sir Robert stormed up the big staircase and disappeared from view. Trudy looked after him, feeling vastly uncertain of herself; then she caught the eye of her mother as she emerged from the lounge.

'Take no notice of your father, my dear,' she said blandly. 'He probably had a bad day at the hospital. You did perfectly right in asking for protection. Now gentlemen — ' she surveyed the four men — 'what moves do you wish to make?'

'I'm Sergeant Forsythe, madam,' said the p.c. man who had spoken before, 'and I'm in charge of the business. I would like two of my men to patrol the grounds, and one man and myself to stay indoors, always within view — or nearly — of Miss Trudy.'

'Very well. Do as you wish. We have dinner at eight. If you wish to join in — '

'No thank you, madam, but we would like to be at some point where we can see

18

Miss Trudy whilst you have the meal.'

Lady Dawson shrugged. 'I leave it to you. You know how to handle these things better than I do.'

With that she returned into the lounge and Trudy stood waiting and listening whilst Forsythe gave his orders. In response two of the men left by the front door. The other one remained at Forsythe's side.

'What do I do, exactly?' Trudy asked vaguely.

'Whatever you would do in the normal way, miss. Take no notice of us: we're good at being unobtrusive. Certainly nobody will be able to get near you.'

'I see.' Trudy wandered towards the lounge. 'I've some reading I want to catch up on before I dress for dinner.'

'Very good, miss.'

And thereafter, though she was always conscious of the p.c. men hovering around, Trudy pursued her usual habits — but not entirely. All the time she was trying to shake off a growing drowsiness, which she could only put down to the after-effects of her hectic party the night before. In catching up on her romantic novel she nearly fell asleep, until the sound of her father's voice sharply awakened her.

'See what you've got us into, Trudy?' he demanded, as he came into the lounge and saw the p.c. men lounging near the window. 'Good as made us prisoners in our own home!'

'Don't be ridiculous, Robert,' his wife admonished. 'On the contrary you ought to be glad Trudy had the commonsense to tackle the danger — if any — in the right way.'

'Huh!' the famous surgeon growled; and thereafter it was hard for either Trudy or his wife to get a word out of him. Things livened up somewhat when June came in from a long afternoon of shopping, mainly because she was the kind of girl who refused to indulge in stolid silences.

'So the men of the law are on the job!' she commented, glancing towards the two by the window. 'I was watched and then questioned before I reached the front door. Been a bit of a lark if I couldn't

20

have got into my own home, wouldn't it?'

'Blame your sister for all of it,' Sir Robert growled.

'Blame her? Not I! She told mother and me why she did it, and I thought she showed unusual brains — even if her lengthy explanation did delay me on my shopping tour.'

'Which means you and mother are on my side,' Trudy smiled. 'Good! That makes me feel a lot better. You listening, dad?'

'I can hardly help it, can I?' Sir Robert laid aside his newspaper wearily. 'It's just the — the general atmosphere of the business that irritates me.'

'If there should be anything in the warning Trudy got,' June mused, 'it's been stifled at birth. You ought to be grateful for that, dad.'

With that she left the lounge, obviously not particularly upset either by the warning to her sister, or the presence of the p.c. men. Trudy sat thinking for a moment, then she tried again to get interested in her novel. Yet again she began to doze over it, finally shaking her head irritably.

'I'll get changed for dinner,' she said, getting up. 'Maybe that will freshen me up a bit.'

'Too many late nights and too many parties, my girl,' Sir Robert observed, looking over his glasses. 'Better slow down a bit. I don't want you as a patient, remember.'

Trudy stifled a yawn, made no answer, and left the lounge. Silently the p.c. men followed her, later taking up position outside the door of her bedroom. Forsythe glanced at his watch and made a wry face.

'Ten past seven,' he said. 'Another two hours, Jerry, and our job's finished.'

The other nodded and stifled a yawn. 'Who'd be a policeman? No excitement and no glamour!'

Bored with their task, but nevertheless rigid adherents of duty, they continued to wait. Meanwhile Trudy, within her room, dressed leisurely for dinner — a custom which she would much rather have abandoned, had it not been for the somewhat old fashioned, traditional ideas of her father. For Sir Robert believed firmly in old customs, and nothing could shake him. Only when some hospital call kept him away from dinner did the family dress and behave as they liked . . .

At twenty minutes to eight Trudy emerged again into the corridor, looking pretty but still tired. Her eyes lacked any sparkle, even though cosmetics gave her plenty of color.

'Everything in order, Miss Dawson?' Forsythe asked, more for the sake of something to say than anything else.

Trudy smiled at him. 'Yes, everything. And, you know, I do apologize for making demands on you gentlemen in this way, but I — '

'Think nothing of it,' Forsythe interrupted. 'It's our job, and that's the end of it — '

'Trudy!' called a voice from the hall. 'Trudy, are you coming down?'

'That's my sister,' Trudy said quietly, sweeping past with a vague hint of tantalizing perfume. 'Excuse me . . . '

Stolidly Forsythe and his colleague followed her along the corridor and down the big staircase. At the base of the stairs they paused, trying not to look as they beheld her in the affectionate embrace of a tall, black-haired young man. Then, as she detached herself and glanced towards the stairs, she evidently realized she had some explanation to make.

'This — this is Dr. Herbert Mason,' she said quickly. 'My fiancé.'

The black haired young man, immaculate in evening dress, inclined his head slightly and then looked puzzled.

'Who are these gentlemen, Trudy?' he inquired.

'Come into the lounge and I'll tell you.'

Mason nodded, gave another surprised glance, and then followed Trudy out of sight. Relentlessly Forsythe and his partner followed her up, took their positions at the far end of the family, and as near as possible detached themselves from the proceedings.

Obviously this was the gathering of the family before dinner should be announced. Everyone was present — Sir Robert and his wife, June, Trudy, and Dr. Mason. Every one of them in evening dress and, at the moment, all of them chatting . . . Then after a moment June detached herself and came across the lounge.

'Wouldn't you two watchdogs like a drink?' she asked, her left eyebrow up in something like amusement.

'No thanks, miss, not while we're on duty,' Forsythe replied.

'Then — er — would you care to join us at dinner — '

'No thanks, miss. Your mother made that suggestion, but when we're on duty we have to refuse.'

'Too bad. You want to be sociable, yet regulations won't permit of it.'

'That's about the size of it, miss,' Forsythe agreed rather woodenly.

June hesitated over something, and Forsythe summed her up professionally. As a man, he liked her well enough. She was some inches taller than Trudy, with fair hair and hazel eyes. Pretty, after a fashion, yet marred somewhat by her rather overdone sophistication. She was probably in the late twenties, yet tried to affect a manner appropriate to the forties. Otherwise she was pleasing enough.

'No regulation against talking to you, is

there?' she asked, after a moment.

'None, miss.'

'Good. I've nobody else to talk to at the moment. Dad and I never did see eye to eye, and Trudy's got her beloved Herbert to concentrate on. And mother — Well, she sort of referees. Keeps dad in order, so to speak. Gerald was the one I used to talk to and argue with. We were two of a pair.'

'Gerald?'

'Yes — my brother, you know. Things haven't been the same for me since he died.'

'I see,' Forsythe said stolidly, who was not aware of the Gerald Dawson facts.

'I suppose you're wondering who the odd man out is?' June continued, glancing towards young Dr. Mason as he talked urgently to an attentively listening Trudy.

'We know he's your sister's fiancé,' Forsythe said. 'She told us that much.'

'Oh — then there's not much left for me to tell. He and Trudy plan to get married in the spring — and a good match too, I should think. He's a hypnotherapist in the same hospital as dad, and according to dad he's a genius.

Going to make his mark with his new method of treatment.'

'Hypnotherapy?' Forsythe repeated, pondering. 'Anything to do with hypnotic surgery and so forth?'

'I believe so. Hypnosis instead of anaesthetic, and all that kind of thing. Herbert's quite an expert at it, and since he's only about thirty he ought to have a brilliant career before — '

June broke off as the maid appeared and announced that dinner was ready. Conversation ceased forthwith as the family and Dr. Mason moved out of the lounge. Forsythe glanced at his colleague.

'To smell and see a good dinner and be forced to stand aside is going to be hell,' he commented. 'I've a damned good mind to change my job.'

He glanced at his watch, observed that it was precisely eight o'clock, and then having entered the dining room he moved over to an unobtrusive position with his colleague and proceeded to keep an eye on the proceedings.

Not that there was anything spectacular. There was a constant flow of conversation and plenty of good food — In other words, a perfectly normal well-to-do family dining in the traditional manner. Certainly no hint of death in the air, even though Trudy was increasingly conscious of the threat that had been made to her as the gap to nine o'clock began to narrow.

Her nervousness was plain to be seen. It expressed itself in her heightened color, her quick breathing, and her never ending prattling. It just could not be called conversation. She rattled on with the inconsequence and vagueness of a child, and most of the time it was young Dr. Mason to whom she addressed herself. Politely, consolingly, gently he listened to her, making some remark of his own here and there. He typified both the affectionate fiancé and the professional doctor, trying to soothe and commiserate with Trudy at one end the same time. Knowing all the facts, he had an insight into her state of mind.

'This will never do!' he said finally, forcing Trudy to be quiet for a moment. 'Any more of this worked-up, emotional state and you'll have hysterics, Trudy. You have got to control yourself.'

'I can't — somehow,' Trudy whispered, the color still very high beneath the rouge. 'I just can't! You all know what's worrying me! I ask you — would *you* be calm and unconcerned in the same circumstances — ?'

Stopping abruptly, she pointed to the electric clock on the wall.

'Look at the time! Half past eight! And in half an hour I am supposed to die!'

'Oh, forget it!' June exclaimed sharply. 'Just a silly joke — a beastly joke. There's no need to get worked up.'

'Certainly there isn't,' Sir Robert said flatly. 'Let's have no more of it, Trudy! You're behaving like a silly child. It would be bad enough in the ordinary way, but with these two gentlemen from Scotland Yard looking on as well it becomes positively embarrassing. Stop it!'

The blunt authority in the voice seemed to have some effect. With a tremendous effort Trudy took a grip on herself, made an end of her meal, and then got to her feet.

'I'll — I'll perhaps feel better in the lounge,' she said; and immediately Mason too had risen and taken her arm. Silently, Forsythe and his colleague got on the move too.

Thereafter, as the rest of the family came in one by one and disported themselves in various chairs, Trudy kept her eyes almost unceasingly on the clock as the finger crept up to nine. She was not doing much talking now but gave the impression of being inwardly overwhelmed by panic thoughts. On the arm of the chair Mason was perched, holding the girl in a protective grip.

'There's absolutely nothing to worry about,' he murmured. 'In a moment or two it will be nine o'clock — and quite obviously there isn't an enemy within miles of you. You're surrounded by your own family: over there are the two men from Scotland Yard to protect you. Security on every side.'

'I know, I know, but — ' Trudy leapt in restless anxiety to her feet. 'Still there is this feeling of uncertainty — an awful presentiment . . . '

She swung, wide-eyed, as though she had seen something that nobody else could see. She was apparently looking at the clock — yet somehow through its ornamental design to the oak-panelled well beyond.

'Nine o'clock,' she whispered, dry lipped, as the hour began to strike. 'I — I — '

She gulped and struggled for words, took a faltering step forward, then suddenly her knees gave way and she collapsed full length to the skin rug.

For an instant there was dead silence. The rest of the family, which included Mason, were on their feet, astounded. Before they could even move Forsythe hurtled across from his corner and dropped to his knees. He took the girl's wrist in finger and thumb. He listened intently to her breast . . . Then he very slowly looked up.

'Dead,' he said quietly, as the last gonging stroke of nine faded into silence.

2

In Chief-Inspector Hargraves' office there was comparative silence. It was just twelve hours since Trudy had died. Nine in the morning, with the dingy view of the Embankment outside the office window, and a slow drift of drizzle over the autumn scene.

'And that's how it happened, sir,' Forsythe said, seated at the desk. 'The Divisional Inspector thought I should let you have the details personally. There's little more to add to the official report which I delivered here last night.'

'On the contrary,' Hargraves said grimly, turning. 'There is a great deal more! Trudy Dawson was murdered . . . That is if we dispense with the conception of suicide.'

'But that isn't possible, sir! There was nobody in the room except the family, and her fiancé. Or perhaps you mean that her general emotional state brought on heart failure?'

'I mean that she was poisoned!' Hargraves came across to the desk and picked up a sheet of paper. 'Here is the post mortem report. Rightly, on Trudy's death, you informed the Divisional Inspector and he ordered a post-mortem in readiness for the coroner. This report means the coroner will simply adjourn the inquest whilst we make inquiries . . . Read it for yourself.'

Forsythe took the report and scanned it:

For the attention of C.I. Hargraves.
Report on Trudy Dawson, Deceased.

It is plain from preliminary post-mortem examination that the deceased died from a heavy dose of hyoscyamus, though the exact time of it being administered is difficult to determine. When one considers the various strengths of hyoscyamus, one has also to allow varying times for its peak effect, which could be anything from twenty-four hours to a few minutes. This

33

depends upon the dilution of the poison, the quantity used, and so forth. The final effects of the poison are intense excitement, dry mouth, thirst, dilated pupils, and then sudden death.

Boyd Lester.
Divisional Surgeon.

'Hyoscyamus is in the atropine and belladonna group. I know that much,' Forsythe said, tossing the report down on the desk. 'But that's all I *do* know — Anyway, when was it administered? At dinner?'

Hargraves shrugged. 'No idea. But we'll find out . . . the lounge and dining room have been sealed off pending investigation, I understand?'

'Yes, sir. The Divisional-Inspector ordered it until after the post-mortem. If Trudy had died from natural causes that would end the matter . . . but now I guess the matter passes to you.'

'Right.' Hargraves sat at his desk and made an irritated movement. 'If only I'd taken more notice of that girl's presentiment! She knew — instinctively — that trouble was coming to her!'

'Can't blame yourself for that, sir,' Brice said, seated at his desk. 'We can't rely on presentiments: only facts.'

'Yes, how true.' Hargraves gave a sigh; then he alerted again. 'We'll start getting busy right away — but first of all, Forsythe, I'd like an amplification of this report of yours. You say that Trudy did not behave rationally in the hour before she died?'

'No, sir. Now I've seen the medical report I know why. It was obviously the effect of the poison. She was extremely talkative, very excited, and nearly on the verge of hysterics. Dr. Mason, her fiancé, did all he could to — '

'Dr. Mason?'

'Yes, sir. It's all there in the report. He's a hypnotherapist in the same hospital as Sir Robert Dawson.'

'I see.' Hargraves thought for a moment, then glanced through the rest of the report. 'All right, Forsythe. Thanks. I'll be in touch again if anything more puzzles me.'

Forsythe nodded and went on his way.

Hargraves continued to glance through the report, then he looked across at Brice who was waiting attentively.

'I don't like it,' Hargraves said, his mouth setting. 'This was cold-blooded murder, and anybody who'd murder a nice girl like Trudy Dawson has a lot to answer for . . . in fact it's perhaps *two* murders,' he finished, musing.

'Two?' Brice raised his eyebrows.

'Yes. Didn't Trudy tell us that her brother had died at nine o'clock in a motor smash not long ago? I thought then it was coincidence: now I'm beginning to wonder. Anyway, we've got to get busy. Tell the fingerprint boys and photographers to get ready and we'll start moving.'

So, towards ten o'clock, the full panoply of the law descended on the Dawson residence. Every detail was recorded, true to police routine, then Hargraves set about the task of interrogation. This presented no problem since all the family was present — even Sir Robert, who was far too upset by the death of his daughter to think about his normal work.

One by one, in the privacy of the study, Hargraves instituted a cross-examination of the family, Sergeant Brice taking everything down in shorthand. The last one to be interviewed was Sir Robert himself, unusually quiet and clearly depressed.

'I realize how you must be feeling at this time, Sir Robert,' Hargraves said quietly. 'Naturally I will try to make things as easy as possible for you — but you will appreciate that I must have every fact if I am to get at the truth.'

'Naturally,' Dawson agreed. 'I'll help out as far as I can.'

'Good. Then tell me this: You are a doctor of considerable renown. You know now that your daughter was killed by hyoscyamus. Did you not recognize symptoms of poisoning in her general behavior prior to her death?'

Dawson shrugged. 'Had I been alert for them I certainly should have done so — but having no reason to suspect anything of the kind I just assumed that she was in a highly emotional state, which considering the circumstances was not to be wondered at.'

'Quite so . . . It would seem that Trudy had a bitter enemy. Have you any idea who this might be?'

'Not the remotest, inspector. As far as I know, Trudy was liked by everybody. She never mentioned any enemies. I could better imagine June having enemies than her — people who might resent her sophisticated attitude, if you understand me. No, Trudy was a happy girl — a good-time girl in fact, and as you will have gathered she was all locked up in her forthcoming marriage to Herbert Mason.'

'Quite . . . ' Hargraves reflected for a moment. 'Concerning this Dr. Mason: could you give me a few more facts about him? I know he's at the same hospital as yourself, but there my information ends.'

'He's been at the hospital for about two years,' Dawson said. 'He met Trudy about a year ago and they became engaged just recently. I gave their engagement my blessing since I know Herbert intimately. He's a clever man at his work, and privately he's the complete gentleman.'

'He's a hypnotherapist, I believe?'

'That is so. He's doing great work in the field.'

'Mmmm. There are a few things more I'd like to know about him, but that's a matter for he himself to attend to. I take it I can reach him at St. Luke's Hospital?'

Dawson nodded. 'Any time. He's the resident hypnotherapist.'

Hargraves got to his feet and strolled round the big study for a while before he asked another question.

'Have you any enemies that you know of, Sir Robert?'

'Enemies?' The surgeon looked vaguely surprised. 'I don't know about that, but I daresay there are plenty of people who don't like me. The jealous ones, for instance — which are inseparable from a profession like mine. Or maybe there are some people who are a little piqued because I've failed in this or that operation. Not,' Dawson added, 'that I can see what that has to do with the murder of Trudy.'

'In confidence, Sir Robert, I begin to suspect that Trudy was not the only one to be murdered. What about your son Gerald?'

'But that was a motor smash.'

'Perhaps . . . The point I'm making is this. Perhaps some person has notions about revenge upon you — but instead of taking that revenge upon you personally it is falling on those who are near and dear to you. There is nothing unique about the idea: there have been cases of it before.'

'But I still don't see how Gerald's smash and Trudy's murder can be interlinked.'

'They both happened at nine o'clock. It may be coincidence: on the other hand it may not. I'm going to make it my business to find out, because if they were both deliberately murdered our viewpoint shifts. We begin to see that the murders have not an individual reason, but are part of something larger. Something which may involve the whole family if it isn't stopped.'

'You can't throw any light on the incidents immediately prior to your son's death, I suppose?' Hargraves continued, as the surgeon remained grimly silent.

'No, I'm afraid not.' Dawson forced himself to attention. 'I was away at the hospital all day and evening. In fact I believe June was the last one to see him as he left the house prior to his fatal accident.'

'He didn't perhaps receive a mysterious death warning?'

Dawson started. 'I've no idea: such a thought never occurred to any of us. If he did, I assume it would be by telephone. The maid might know something.'

Hargraves moved over to the bell-push and depressed it. Then he stood thoughtfully waiting until the maid arrived. She was entirely respectful, but obviously nervous.

'Yes, sir?'

'I want you tell me something, if you can — er — '

'My name's Baines, sir.'

'Thank you. You know, of course, why I am here — conducting an inquiry into the mysterious death of Miss Trudy. I have reason to believe there may be an offshoot to the matter in connection with Mr. Gerald.'

'I understand, sir.'

'I want you to think back, Baines — very carefully. Before Mr. Gerald went out on the evening of his death, can you recall if he received a 'phone call?'

Baines nodded promptly. 'Yes, sir — about twenty to eight.'

'You seem very sure of this, Baines,' Hargraves murmured.

'Only because it is part of my job to answer the 'phone, sir. Somebody asked for Mr. Gerald, so naturally I put the call through to his room.'

'And he answered?'

'Almost immediately, sir.'

'You don't happen to know what the call was about, I suppose?' The maid looked faintly indignant. 'Certainly not, sir. When Mr. Gerald answered I put the 'phone back on its cradle.'

'I see.' Hargraves smiled a little. 'Have no fear, Baines: I am perfectly sure you behaved properly — but on this occasion it might have helped us had you not done so. Incidentally, you mentioned this at the inquest on Mr. Gerald, I suppose?'

'Why, no!' The girl looked worried.

42

'Should I have done so? Nobody asked me. I never thought — '

'Never mind; it's passed now,' Hargraves interrupted. 'Let us go back for a moment. What kind of a voice had this caller? What did he say? Incidentally, I suppose it *was* a man?'

'Oh yes, sir, it was a man all right. He had a — a very soft, gentle voice. Sort of soothing, it was.'

'Mmmm. Can you recall what he said?'

'He simply asked for Mr. Gerald Dawson — nothing more.'

Hargraves nodded. 'All right, Baines: that's all I need to know. You can go.'

The girl departed and for a moment Hargraves stood in silence; then he glanced across at Sir Robert.

'I think we may safely assume, Sir Robert, that your son received a telephone warning, just the same as Trudy did. The only difference was that there was not as much time lag between warning and event — and of course the fact that your son apparently did not take any precautions, like calling for police protection, for instance.'

'Why on earth do you suppose he suddenly decided to head for the south coast?' the surgeon asked, puzzled. 'And how was it that, despite the decision he had made, he ran into death at nine o'clock just the same? Suppose he'd gone north? Do you think he'd have died just the same?'

'That is one of the imponderables, Sir Robert: I just don't know the answer — yet.' Hargraves moved with sudden action. 'Well, I think I've got all I want here for the moment, Sir Robert. My inquiries will have to branch out a bit since apparently I'm covering two murders instead of one. I think I'll have a word with Dr. Mason next. If anything unusual happens just ring me at the Yard. In the meantime carry on as usual.'

The surgeon rose slowly, his face haggard. 'Thanks for all you're doing, inspector . . . About the funeral, what is the procedure?'

'Normal,' Hargraves said. 'We have all we need now the post-mortem has been made . . . Oh, I would remind you that there is need for care in regard to yourself, your wife, and your daughter June.'

'Care?'

'As I said before, this seems to be a matter aimed at the entire family, and not one person in particular. The rest of you are therefore in danger. Anything, no matter how slight, that gives rise to suspicion should be reported immediately.'

'I'll remember that, inspector.'

Hargraves nodded, shook hands, and then departed with Brice. They were in the police car on their way to St. Luke's hospital, before Brice ventured a comment.

'From the look of things, sir, this business goes a lot deeper than we'd thought at first sight.'

'No doubt of that.'

'Think you'll get anything out of Dr. Mason?'

'No idea. Chiefly I want to find out what his relationship was with Trudy. I know he was engaged to her, but there may have been deeper issues.'

Clearly, Hargraves was not in a particularly communicative mood so Brice let the matter drop. He drove as swiftly as possible through the crowded London streets until he finally reached the sweeping drive-in outside St. Luke's hospital.

'Okay,' Hargraves murmured, opening the car door. 'Let's be going.'

Once they had identified themselves to the reception sister there was no difficulty in obtaining an interview with the young hypnotherapist. The two men were conducted to a private ante-room, and presently the white-coated Mason put in an appearance. He had an air of business about him, but he certainly did not seem perturbed at finding two men of Scotland Yard waiting to see him.

'We're police officers, doctor — ' Hargraves began, displaying his warrant-card; but Mason cut him short.

'Yes, I'm aware of that. The sister told me. I suppose it has something to do with Trudy?'

'Exactly so,' Hargraves assented. 'Routine inquiry, you understand . . . I think you might be able to help us. You have not been told yet what caused the girl's death, have you?'

'No idea.' Mason's lips tightened for a moment. 'There seemed to be no sense in it. Last I remember was that the Divisional Inspector had ordered a post-mortem.'

'Exactly. That post-mortem revealed that Miss Dawson died from poisoning — hyoscyamus. I have the task of trying to determine how it was administered, and by whom.'

'Hyoscyamus,' Mason mused. 'That's one of the narcotic irritants.'

'Yes, it is . . . Tell me, did you observe any opportunity for that drug to be administered last night during dinner?'

Mason shook his head. 'No; I certainly didn't, inspector. But now you have mentioned the cause of death I recollect that all Trudy's symptoms were in conformity with having taken such a drug . . . ' he stopped, thoughtful. 'Come to think of it, I believe the poison might have been administered *before* the evening.'

Hargraves alerted. 'What makes you think that?'

'She told me during conversation that she had been intolerably tired all day, and once or twice caught herself out falling asleep. We just passed it off as reaction after the party we attended the night before. I might remark that I was rather surprised because as a rule Trudy was the kind of girl who could take parties in her stride. She had tremendous energy.'

'I infer from this that hyoscyamus poisoning produces drowsiness?'

'Certainly. I'm not much up in poisons since that isn't my field — but I do know that much.'

'Thank you,' Hargraves said, musing. 'Very interesting. Though you are not an expert in poisons, perhaps you can give me some idea how long it would take a dose of hyoscyamus to do its work?'

Mason shrugged. 'I've no real idea. It would depend on the strength of the dose and the resistance of the victim to it. Resistance would be high in a girl as young as Trudy.'

Hargraves glanced towards Brice who

was in the midst of making his usual shorthand notes — then, after a brief pause, Hargraves started on a different track.

'This party you've referred to, Dr. Mason? Where was it?'

'The Café Criterion — just off the Strand.'

'I know the place . . . Was it a celebration, an evening of fun, or what?'

'A mutual friend of ours — Trudy and me, I mean — threw the party to celebrate his engagement to a socialite. It was quite a big affair.'

'About how many guests?'

'Quite a lot — mainly stage people. David Warlock — the chap who threw the party — is a small time West End actor, and you know what pros are when they throw a party.'

'Was there anybody there whom you would describe as enemy of yourself, or Trudy? Or even of Sir Robert?'

'Good heavens, no!' Mason laughed rather incredulously. 'They were all good friends, full of the party spirit . . . or are you suggesting that somebody there administered the poison?'

'I'm not suggesting anything,' Hargraves answered calmly. 'I am simply exploring possibilities.'

'Then I'm afraid you're up a tree there, inspector. It was a perfectly happy party.'

'By invitation, of course?'

'Yes. By ticket — or rather invitation card.'

Hargraves nodded slowly and seemed to be thinking about something. Then he apparently changed his mind. He picked up his hat from the side table, considered it, then asked another question.

'You know of course that Trudy was warned that she would die? A telephone message?'

'Yes — I know.' Mason was grimly serious now. 'When we first discovered she was dead I jumped to the conclusion that she had had a fatal heart attack due to her emotional upset prior to nine o'clock. Now we know that it was the poison causing the trouble.'

'You can't think of anybody likely to send such a 'phone message, even for a practical joke?'

Mason reflected for a long time, then finally he shook his head

'All right — never mind,' Hargraves said. 'But I don't see any harm in telling you that Trudy's brother, Gerald, had a similar 'phone call before he died in a motor smash on the south coast road.'

Mason looked genuinely astonished. 'He did? But how do you know?'

'The maid told us. She should have given the information at the inquest, but nobody asked her about it — and she's not a girl of immense initiative . . . So you see, doctor, it looks as though whoever killed Trudy also killed Gerald — but the 'how' is the big problem. Anyway, thanks for your help.'

Hargraves put on his hat and moved to the door with Sergeant Brice beside him; then he turned.

'By the way, doctor. How much regard has Sir Robert for his family?'

'That's a bit of an odd question, isn't it?' Mason gave a rather grim smile. 'You don't suspect Sir Robert, surely?'

'I suspect everybody, doctor; that's my job.'

'I see . . . Well, in regard to Sir Robert, I should change my opinion, if I were you. There couldn't be a more devoted husband or kinder father than Sir Robert. At least, that's been my experience.'

'You work in this hospital with him. How do you get along?'

'Fair enough. Sir Robert's quite popular with the staff.'

Hargraves nodded. 'Right! Thanks for the information, doctor. I'll be on my way now. I know where you are if I want you again.'

With that Hargraves shook hands and took his departure. He remained in grim thought as Brice drove back to towards the Yard. On the way they stopped for lunch, which Hargraves ate mostly in silence; then they continued on their way to the gloomy office overlooking the Thames embankment.

'What's the next move, sir?' Brice asked.

'I don't know yet.' Hargraves put hat and coat on the hat stand. 'I've got to think a bit. Get your notes typed out into a report and let me have it quick as you can.'

'Right, sir.'

Hargraves lighted a cigarette, drew at it thoughtfully for a moment or two, and then sat down at his desk. He pulled towards him the photographs that had been made of Trudy's death fall in the lounge; and then the fingerprint report. From the latter it appeared that the prints on glasses, crockery, and various articles of furniture, were those of the family — but of course absolute proof of this could only be obtained by taking the prints of each person for comparison tests.

'And the law does not permit of taking prints without a conviction first,' Hargraves muttered. 'Wonder how many more regulations they can think up to hamper a hard-working policeman?'

'Pardon, sir?' Brice glanced up from his keyboard.

'Nothing — just thinking out loud. Look, sergeant, what strikes you as the most puzzling thing in this case?'

'Well, sir, there are quite a few puzzling points — but most outstanding of the lot is the matter of time. The nine o'clock business. Take Gerald Dawson first — If he had been warned that he would die at nine — and presumably he was — how was the killer so sure that he would meet with a fatal accident at that moment? Again, how did the killer know Gerald was going to take the road he did? Presumably, from what we know now, the smash-up on the road was deliberately planned — and for nine o'clock. What on earth made Gerald go in the right direction? It kind of savors of witchcraft, clairvoyance, or . . . or something.'

'I agree; though I don't think either possibility is likely. Certainly, it would seem that our killer has an all-round knowledge of when and where his victims will die, enough knowledge to tell them beforehand. He even gets away with it with police protection all round, as in the case of Trudy.'

'In that case, sir, I think she was poisoned at the party the night before, and the killer knew how long the poison would take to act on a girl of her physical reactions.'

'I incline to the same belief,' Hargraves

said. 'Somebody was at that party for the especial purpose of poisoning Trudy — and to find that somebody will be no easy job, but we can make a start. Since everybody was by invitation it ought to be possible to get a list of the guests from — er — ' Hargraves snapped his fingers indecisively.

'David Warlock?' Brice suggested.

'That's the fellow. Make a note to track him down — either through the stage managements, the Café Criterion, the telephone directory, or something. Even Actors' Equity could probably give you his address. I don't want to get it direct from Dr. Mason.'

'I'm rather curious, sir. Why not?'

'Because I don't want him to know my moves any more than I can help. Reason: he's a doctor. A hypnotherapist, true, but that wouldn't stop him getting supplies of poison if he wanted them, and no questions asked. We've absolutely nothing to pin on him as yet, but I don't agree with putting him in the picture too much.'

'For that matter, Sir Robert is a doctor too.'

'A fact which had not escaped me,' Hargraves said, stubbing out his cigarette. 'But, as in the case of Dr. Mason, I've no reason for suspecting him of dirty work — yet. If it comes that, I think Sir Robert will have more trouble to face before long — even as I told him.'

Hargraves meditated through an interval, then he said:

'We'd take a definite short cut if we could catch our murdering friend redhanded at the telephone — and unless I'm dead off the mark he'll certainly repeat his actions. Criminals always do. There may yet be one more call — '

Hargraves thought further for a moment and then picked up the telephone.

'Post Office Engineering Section,' he said briefly. 'Get me Larry Hayes.'

There was an interval, then Hargraves spoke again. 'That you, Larry? Hargraves here. Look, I need your special help ... Can you come round and I'll explain ... ? Yes, that's right. Okay, soon as you can.'

Hargraves rang off and glanced across at Brice. 'Maybe a hunch worth playing,' he said. 'Meantime I'll track down David Warlock. You get on with that report.'

'Okay, sir.'

Hargraves picked up the telephone again, and for several minutes was in the midst of making inquiries. It was only when he contacted the Criterion that he got a result. The address of David Warlock was given to him instantly. After that it was a matter of getting Warlock himself — and as it happened he was lucky. The private hotel where Warlock was residing announced that he was in, and in another moment he came to the 'phone.

'The police?' Warlock exclaimed, when Hargraves had identified himself. 'But what do you want with me?'

'Just a matter of routine, sir,' Hargraves said, reflecting how beautifully the man spoke — as became his profession of an actor. 'I believe you gave a party two nights ago at the Café Criterion and invited several guests?'

'Why yes, I did. There was nothing wrong with that, was there? The premises of the Criterion are licensed for — '

'I'm not concerned about that, Mr. Warlock. Just let me do the talking please. I'm inquiring into the murder of Trudy Dawson, about which you probably know.'

There was a gasp. 'Trudy murdered! Murdered, did you say?'

'I did. Evidently you didn't see the stop-press notices in this morning's paper.'

'No I didn't, as a matter of fact.'

'You can read the full report in this evening's papers . . . Now to the matter on hand: Can you supply me with a full list of all the guests present at your celebration party?'

'Sure I can. Take a little time, though. There were nearly a hundred of them.'

'No matter. Just submit the list to me as soon as possible — Chief-Inspector Hargraves, Scotland Yard. I want that list today if at all possible.'

'You can have it in an hour. I'll bring it myself.'

'Fair enough.'

Hargraves rang off and gradually lost himself in thought again as Sergeant

Brice typed energetically in the corner. Then, presently, the arrival of Larry Hayes, the chief telephone engineer, brought an interruption.

'Afternoon, inspector,' he greeted breezily. 'What can I do for you this time?'

'You can explain a few things to my woefully non-technical mind,' Hargraves responded. 'Sit down, Larry. Have a cigarette.'

'Thanks.' Hayes lighted up and then waited — a keen-faced, short man who had rapidly climbed to the top in his career as an engineer.

'First, I must put you in the picture,' Hargraves said. 'It's a case of murder — possibly two murders. You'll read the bare facts later in the press . . . To cut it short, a girl named Trudy Dawson, and her brother Gerald, have both been murdered. Where you come in is that they were informed beforehand, by telephone, when the murder would happen . . . Now, to trace a call from a dial phone is impossible. I have reason to think there will be more attempts at murder yet and I want to nab the person sending the telephone warning. How do I do it?'

'You don't know if the warning came from a telephone box, I suppose?'

'I haven't the least idea.'

'Mmmm.' Hayes pondered for a moment and then asked a question. 'What's the telephone set-up at the receiving end?'

'It's on the automatic line.'

'Yes, yes. Practically all 'phones are automatic these days. I mean are there extensions and so forth?'

'There is one main 'phone in the hall, and extensions to every bedroom.'

'It isn't a party line, shared with somebody else?'

No — direct. It's the residence of Sir Robert Dawson, the resident surgeon to St. Luke's hospital.'

'I see. Is there a direct line from the hospital for emergency calls?'

Hargraves shook his head. 'No. Just the normal line.'

'Then that makes it simpler,' Hayes mused. 'We can concentrate on the main incoming line. What we can do, inspector, is have some men use an electronic detector hitched to the main line. When a call comes through one can tell from the strength of the signal, and the direction, the approximate point of origin. It isn't foolproof by any means, but it will give you the source of origin within, say, five miles.'

'You can't narrow the field a little? Five miles is the hell of a lot of territory to cover to pinpoint one caller — and murder could be done in the interval.'

Hayes shrugged. 'Sorry, inspector, but that's the best I can promise. In some ways the automatic exchange has proved a bit of a drawback to the law.'

'You're telling me!' Hargraves growled.

'There's one other way,' Hayes said, pondering further. 'It would be surer, but it's damned complicated. It would mean several men on night and day watch at the telephone exchange — '

'Okay if we have to,' Hargraves said. 'What's the angle?'

'The unit containing the Dawson number would have to be watched, and every time it started to function from an incoming call we should have to trace it.

We could do it by the pulsations and discover the exact source — But like I said, it's complicated.'

'Nothing's so complicated when you're trying to catch a murderer and prevent a further murder,' Hargraves said. 'Do that, Larry, and I will satisfy the Postmaster General if it be necessary. If he won't believe me, I don't doubt the Assistant Commissioner will be able to reassure him.'

Hayes nodded and got to his feet. 'Sir Robert Dawson, you say? Okay — we'll get his number.'

'And don't advise him, or anybody else, of what you're doing,' Hargraves added, as he accompanied the engineer to the door. 'Absolute secrecy is essential, and the same goes for the men employed on the job.'

'Rely on us,' Hayes smiled. We've helped the Yard before and we know how to keep our mouths shut.'

3

Hardly had Larry Hayes departed before David Warlock presented himself. He looked far more like a businessman than an actor, neatly dressed in a pin stripe suit and with polished hair drawn back from his forehead. He was good looking in a theatrical kind of way, and obviously a man of constant alertness.

'Glad to know you, Mr. Warlock,' Hargraves said, shaking hands and drawing forth a chair. 'And I appreciate your promptness in complying with my request.'

'Glad to help.' Warlock seated himself and pulled a list from his breast pocket, laying it on the desk. 'Here it is, inspector. The full list of guests.'

Hargraves read it through briefly, and gave no evidence of the surprise he felt that Warlock had been thorough enough to put not only the names of the guests but their theatrical professions as well. In consequence there were listed 'Dancers,' 'Tumblers,' 'Magician,' 'Singer,' and so forth.

'That do?' Warlock asked, after a while — and Hargraves nodded slowly.

'It will do excellently, Mr. Warlock. Might I ask what prompted you to be so — well, explicit?'

'I simply thought it might help if you knew what each guest was. You like every detail you can get in a matter like this, don't you? Trudy Dawson was a great friend of mine — same as Herbert Mason. I'm as anxious as anybody that you should find the murderer.'

'You know all the people on this guest list quite well?' Hargraves asked, still studying it.

'Some well — and some not so well, but I've been connected with them at some time or other in the course of my profession. Before I became an actor I was in a circus as a marksman — You know, performing almost impossible feats with a rifle; and that's how I came to meet these folks. At the engagement party I simply renewed their acquaintance.'

'I understand . . . There was nobody there whom you didn't know, I suppose? No gate-crashers?'

'No; everybody was accounted for, and I'll vouch for each one of them personally.'

Hargraves smiled. 'You're taking on a load of responsibility, Mr. Warlock. Vouching for close on a hundred people is not a thing to be taken lightly.'

'No, I suppose not, but — ' Warlock paused for a moment and frowned. 'You say Trudy Dawson was murdered. Would I be out of line if I asked how?'

'She was poisoned, Mr. Warlock — and I have reasons for thinking that the poison was perhaps administered during the party — hence the checkup of guests.'

'I can understand that — but it's quite ridiculous, you know. Trudy and Herbert hardly knew any of the guests — at least not when the party started. Not one of them could have any wish to kill her. It's fantastic!'

'Murder is always fantastic,' Hargraves sighed. 'Anyway, thanks for your co-operation, Mr. Warlock. This list will be extremely useful — Oh, by the way, you're an actor, I understand?'

'Correct. Nothing more than juvenile lead as yet, but I have hopes.'

'Good!' Hargraves seemed to consider something, and then rejected it. He held out his hand. 'Best of luck in your career, Mr. Warlock — and if I should need you again I'll contact you.'

Warlock went on his way, and Hargraves slowly closed the office door. Sergeant Brice glanced towards him.

'Seems a genuine enough fellow, sir.'

'On the face of it, yes,' Hargraves agreed, settling at his desk again. 'There's only one thing — Actors are sometimes inclined to carry their profession into real life. Just a thought. I learned long ago never to accept anybody at their face value.'

Brice said no more, and Hargraves set about the long task of sorting out Warlock's guest list. In all there were ninety-two guests, every one of them connected with the theatrical profession. There seemed to be every type from trapeze artistes to hypnotists and thought-readers. At the end of his compilation

Hargraves gave a yawn and lighted a cigarette.

'Better send out for some sandwiches,' he said, glancing at Brice. 'I've a lot more to do yet.'

'Okay, sir.' Brice glanced at the list, with the addresses attached to each name. 'What do you intend doing with that lot, sir?'

'I'm going to toothcomb through them and decide which ones want interviewing first. All of them may have to be interviewed before we're through with this business. I'm convinced that somewhere in this list is the person we want . . . The only thing that will save us a lot of trouble is some fast action by the telephone authorities.'

'Yes, sir. Otherwise it looks as though we've got a job for life!'

* * *

For some days afterwards nothing untoward took place. Trudy Dawson was buried, and thereafter a grim calm settled over the family. The inquest was adjourned

67

at Hargraves' request, pending further police investigation. He himself, with his men, strained every nerve to fit the pieces into the puzzle.

He was working now on two murders — satisfied in his own mind that Gerald Dawson had met his death by some carefully planned, clever trick. He went to the actual spot where Gerald's car had plunged to destruction, examined the road carefully and read the police reports — yet there was not a single clue that gave any indication as to why Gerald had suddenly plunged off the road to his death.

Then suddenly — the threat of disaster yet again! Hargraves was in his office in mid-afternoon, trying to think some sense into the Dawson mystery, when the telephone suddenly shrilled. Mechanically he reached out to the instrument.

'Hargraves speaking,' he said, his eyes on his notes.

'Larry Hayes here,' came the swift answer. 'You'd better move fast, chief: A warning's just come through to Dawson, and we heard every word of it — '

'You got the location of the call?' Hargraves demanded.

'Yes. Belgrave Court, 4690. That's a call box situated at the corner of Belgrave Court.'

'I'll call you back,' Hargraves said quickly. He waited only a fraction for the line to clear, then made contact with the radio room. 'Send out a call to all cars in the Belgrave Court area. Proceed immediately to call box at the corner of Belgrave Court and investigate anybody who had just finished a call on the telephone. I'll follow it up.'

He put the 'phone back, leapt up, and scrambled into his hat and coat. Brice also moved fast, guessing what was coming, and within seconds they were in the fast squad car, racing through the traffic.

As it happened, Belgrave Court was not very far from the Yard. It formed a small enclosure, crescent shaped, the horns of the crescent being bounded by the main road — Elmington Crescent. It was as they raced towards their rendezvous that Hargraves began to frown to himself.

'Y'know something, sergeant?' he said presently. 'There's a squad car on permanent duty on Elmington Crescent, enforcing speed laws. Maybe we'll be lucky with that car right on the spot.'

Brice nodded briefly, his mind on the job of driving. In something like ten minutes he reached Elmington Crescent, raced down it, then swung into Belgrave Court and came to a stop. Hargraves clicked the door latch and leapt out. Two squad cars were already there, drawn up beside the telephone box.

'Well?' Hargraves demanded, as the men saluted.

'Two cars making inquiries, sir,' the patrol sergeant said. 'We've been here quite a time. I can't see what use inquiries are — with all respect — because nobody has used this box for the last half hour.'

Hargraves stared in amazement for a moment; then he quickly stepped into the 'phone box and looked at the number under the telephone rest. It was the one Larry Hayes had given him — 4690 . . . Slowly Hargraves emerged again.

'Nobody in the last half hour?' he

repeated, going back to the patrol sergeant.

'That's right, sir. We've been within sight of this box since lunchtime, on patrol traffic duty. We were a bit surprised when we got your radio message. Three patrols came up within minutes. Two of them set off to inquire of all people in this section, and the remaining one stopped here with us.'

Hargraves cuffed his hat up on to his forehead and gave Brice a look,

'Doesn't make sense, sir,' Brice said. 'Maybe Hayes got his facts wrong somewhere.'

'Soon find out,' Hargraves said, as a Post Office 'phone van turned into the Court. Here's Hayes now, I think.'

He was correct. The van stopped and Larry Hayes came hurrying across, then he slowed his pace as he saw the expression on Hargraves' face.

'You slipped up, Larry,' Hargraves growled. 'Nobody's used this box in the last half hour.'

Hayes frowned. 'But they must have done! There's no slip-up in our department. Dawson's automatic 'phone was actuated by a call coming from this box.

Dammit, we heard — and tape recorded — the speaker.'

'You did record him? Good! What did he say?'

'He asked first for Sir Robert Dawson. There was a long pause, and no immediate answer even when Dawson spoke. Then after a moment the caller said —' Hayes pulled a note from his pocket. 'He said 'I have a message for you, Sir Robert. I will make it as brief as possible. You will die at precisely nine o'clock tonight. Good bye.' Then he rang off.'

'Exactly the same as Trudy's warning,' Hargraves muttered. 'And probably the same as Gerald's warning too. Yet nobody was seen here at this box! See here, Larry, could the call have been made by some other method, and yet seem to come from here? Could a 'phone be hitched to the Dawson wire, for instance? Say — over waste land or something?'

'It could; but then you wouldn't get a reaction from his number.' Hayes looked dogged. 'In spite of everything I say the call came from here, and from this number.'

Hargraves tightened his mouth and then came to a decision.

'We've got to hop to the Dawson residence right away, and leave this telephone puzzle until later.' He looked at the patrol sergeant. 'Have the other men report any information to my office . . . Let's go.'

Hargraves raced for his car with Brice close behind him; and once they were settled Brice wasted no time in covering the journey to the Dawson residence.

'Everything else apart, sir,' he said, as he drove steadily, 'and by that I mean the mystery of the 'phone box — doesn't it strike you as a bit queer that Sir Robert should be at home at this time of day to receive the call? I thought he was a resident surgeon at the hospital.'

'Normally, yes.' Hargraves made an irritated gesture. 'It would suggest that the caller knows exactly when his victim is at home, and when he is not. Add that to a telephone box which nobody has visited during the critical time, and where are we?'

It was plain that Hargraves was on edge

— and certainly not without reason — so Brice kept his counsel and said no more. He completed the journey to the Dawson home in record time and pulled up with a jerk outside the front door.

'I'm extremely glad you've come, gentlemen,' Sir Robert said urgently, as the maid showed them into the lounge. 'I have been trying to get you on the 'phone, inspector. I've had a warning from — '

'Yes, I know,' Hargraves interposed. 'A warning identical to that received by your late daughter.'

'You know?' The surgeon looked surprised. 'How does that come about?'

'The exact details don't matter, Sir Robert. Let me have the facts, please.'

The obviously worried surgeon motioned to the settee, and then seated himself in the armchair opposite. Hargraves, eyeing him intently, could not help but notice the curious faraway look in his eyes and the general harassment on his features.

'I've been at home all today,' he explained. 'I haven't felt too well. Then this afternoon that 'phone call came through.'

'Did the maid take it in the first instance?' Hargraves asked quickly.

'Yes. Do you want to see her?'

'It might help. I must have every detail.'

Sir Robert rose and rang the bell. In a moment or two the maid arrived.

'Just a question, Baines,' Hargraves said. 'You took a telephone call for Sir Robert this afternoon?'

'Yes, sir. Be about half — '

'Never mind the time. What did the caller say?'

'He asked for Sir Robert, so I put the call through to Sir Robert's bedroom. He was resting.'

'Would you say the voice was the same one that called Mr. Gerald before he met his death?'

The girl hesitated for a moment and then slowly nodded.

'Yes, I think it was. And also the same one that called Miss Trudy.'

Hargraves glanced. 'Then you were the first to receive that call, too?'

'Yes, inspector. I've not said anything because — Well, as I said before when you questioned me: nobody asked me.'

Hargraves nodded slowly. 'I see. Each time the caller has asked for a certain party, and you have then switched the 'phone through on the extension?'

'That's it, sir. I would be willing to swear on a Bible that the voice was identical every time. A sort of soft voice — a man's — and kind of soothing . . . '

'Yes, Baines, so you said before. Right — that's all, thank you.'

For the briefest instant the girl hesitated as though she were about to add something further; then evidently thinking better of it she quietly left the room.

'Well, there it is,' Sir Robert said, spreading his hands. 'Baines told me this unknown caller was on the line, and at first I rather doubted it because there was a long delay before he finally spoke. Then, without giving me a chance to speak or ask a question he told me that I was going to die at nine tonight . . . I took the message down whilst it was still fresh in my mind. Here it is.'

The surgeon pulled a scrap of paper from his pocket and handed it over. Hargraves read it through and then pocketed it. As he knew already, it was identical to the message received by Trudy — and probably Gerald as well.

'So what do I do now?' the surgeon asked grimly, and Hargraves jerked himself out of a spell of thought.

'Obviously, Sir Robert, you must have protection.'

'I see . . . You know I dislike it intensely. And, forgive me, it doesn't seem to be much use. At least not as far as Trudy was concerned.'

'We can only do our best,' Hargraves shrugged. 'I'll have a couple of men sent along right away, and they will keep a constant watch . . . Tell me, what are your plans for the rest of today?'

'Nothing very formidable. As I say, I haven't been feeling too well, and I don't intend to go out for the rest of today. The hospital knows I'm indisposed, so I'll have no calls from that direction. I had planned to rest for the remainder of today, take a bath this evening, and then go to bed.'

'Which will make you an easy subject to guard,' Hargraves smiled. 'What about the rest of the family? What are they doing? Or intend to do?'

'I can't answer for them, I'm afraid. My wife is out at the moment at a meeting; and June has gone shopping. They'll probably be at home for the evening.'

'I would prefer that they *are*,' Hargraves said decisively. 'Tell them that is my wish, Sir Robert — and as to the rest try not to worry too much. We're still working hard on this business, you know — but of course the killer has a head start on us and it takes time.'

'Yes — I understand.' Sir Robert rose to his feet as Hargraves and Brice got up. 'I understand now exactly how poor Trudy felt as nine o'clock came closer.'

'A lot of her excitement and alternating depression was the work of poison,' Hargraves reminded. 'I don't think that is the case with you.'

The faraway look came and went in Sir Robert's eyes. He did not answer the remark; instead he held out his hand rather woodenly.

'I'll see you are looked after,' Hargraves promised, and then he went on his way with Brice behind him . . .

As he drove back to the Yard, Brice cast a sideways look at his superior's thoughtful face.

'You didn't tell him that nobody had been in the 'phone box to call him, sir.'

'Correct. I'd hardly be such a damn fool as to do that. It's quite plain he hasn't much faith in the police as it is; no sense in piling on the agony.'

'How about that maid, sir? Think she's got anything to do with it?'

'She's on the list of suspects, same as all of them are — but if you want my personal opinion I don't think she's a thing to do with it. She just happens to be one of those irritating sort of people who never say anything unless they are directly questioned. They're the bane of a policeman's life.'

Brice drove on in silence for a while; then Hargraves presently spoke again.

'There's an interesting point in regard to the messages, sergeant, even if I don't see the connection as yet. Every time, between the first contact and the second, there was a big delay. I mean — first

Baines got the call; then before anybody spoke to the actual person such as Trudy, Sir Robert, or even Gerald, there was a long delay. Trudy mentioned it, and now her father does the same thing . . . And there is something else. The caller never gives a chance to ask a question. He simply makes a statement and rings off, without apparently satisfying himself that the person has got the call.'

'Mmm, that's true enough,' Brice admitted. 'I know I always ask the person to identify himself, or herself, before I start speaking.'

'So does anybody, as a rule. That's what makes it so odd.'

'Even more odd when apparently nobody calls at all!' Brice growled. 'At the end of all this we just have an empty phone-box. The business doesn't even begin to make sense.'

Hargraves did not say anything. He followed up a line of thought of his own — and was still following it when Scotland Yard was reached once more.

He did not say what conclusion he had come to. His first move on reaching the office was to detail a couple of p.c. men to guard duty at the Dawson residence. This done, he picked up a report from his desk and studied it.

'We're getting nowhere fast!' he commented, tossing the report over to Brice. 'Read that!'

Brice did so, and it did not take him long, either. It stated quite simply that nothing had come of inquiries of people who had used the Belgrave Court telephone kiosk. So far as could be ascertained it not been used at all since early in the morning.

'Damned queer, sir,' Brice commented, pondering. 'It makes it we don't quite know what to do next. If we had ordinary, straightforward murder to deal with we'd know what we're doing, but as it is we're right up a gum tree.'

'Yes — so it would seem,' Hargraves muttered. 'It looks to me as though the only thing we can do at the moment is try and trace something through Warlock's guests. If we can find the poisoner of Trudy, then we've got the prime mover in all the murders.'

'All, sir?' Brice looked surprised. 'Only two so far! Or do you expect that Sir Robert is going to fall a victim as well despite the precautions?'

'I don't *want* to think so, naturally, but somehow — ' Hargraves gave a sigh. 'I just don't know, sergeant! This damned murderer seems to have such an uncanny way of implementing his warnings — yet on the other hand we can't do any more than take every reasonable precaution. Have to leave it at that for the moment, and see what happens tonight.'

* * *

At the Dawson residence, Sir Robert did not take kindly to the idea of surveillance, but since it was a necessary evil he had to put up with it. And, being a physician and surgeon of considerable experience, he did a great deal to help himself — chiefly in the realm of self-analysis. He tested his own physical reactions, made sure there was no poison in his bloodstream, and generally checked up on his reflexes, nerves, and blood pressure. Finally he arrived at the conclusion that he was normal, except for a curious haziness of the mind that he could not altogether analyze.

For some curious reason he had extreme difficulty in remembering what he had done during the morning. There was a gap in his consciousness somewhere which he couldn't fill. It worried him — so much so that he questioned his wife and June about it when they arrived home within a few minutes of each other in the early evening . . . In the background of the lounge, trying to be as unobtrusive as possible, the two p.c. men hovered. By name Sheard and Thompson, they were about the two top men in their particular line — far more efficient than the less keen but well meaning Forsythe and his colleague.

'It seems to me,' June remarked, with her usual air of phony sophistication, 'that this house is becoming a sort of rendezvous for Scotland Yard. What's the idea, dad? This some new idea of Inspector Hargraves?'

'You might as well know — and you

too, Maude — ' Sir Robert glanced at his wife — 'that I received a telephone threat on my life this afternoon whilst you were out. A threat phrased exactly like the warning to Trudy.'

June started in horrified wonder, whilst her mother gave a gasp and raised a hand to her mouth.

'There's no need for panic, or even alarm,' Sir Robert continued grimly. 'These men are on guard, and will continue to remain so until after nine tonight, when — as in the other case of Trudy, and maybe Gerald as well — my demise is supposed to take place. On the other hand I have made a check up, and I can vouch for the fact that I certainly shan't die from poisoning! Nor from a motor smash, since I don't intend going out. Don't worry, either of you: we've got the situation taped.'

'That's what Trudy thought,' his wife said bitterly. 'And yet look what happened!'

'I know . . . Just the same, I am an experienced middle-aged man and alert for every trick. And I don't intend to be caught out.' Sir Robert hesitated for a moment; then, 'I am just a bit puzzled over one thing. My memory doesn't seem to be too bright today. This may sound silly, but do either of you know what I did between ten and eleven this morning?'

'I've not the least idea,' Maude said, after thinking for a moment. 'I know you've been at home all day because you didn't feel too good, but most of the time you were resting.'

'Except for an interval during the morning!' June exclaimed. 'I've just remembered! You came down around ten o'clock, dad, and went out to the garage. You didn't explain yourself, and I certainly didn't think it was my business to ask you. I was in the lounge here and saw you through the window. After maybe five minutes in the garage you came back into the house and went up to the bathroom. You were in there some time, then you came out and went along to your bedroom. We didn't see you again until you came down for lunch.'

The two p.c. mentally recorded everything and waited for the next. It was some time in coming. Sir Robert sat with his lips tight as he tried to fill gaps in his memory — then at last he gave a shrug.

'I just don't know,' he confessed. 'Maybe I need some psychiatric treatment at the hospital for incipient amnesia. I suppose I must have gone to the garage to get something from the car. Then I went to the bathroom to wash my hands, perhaps. So — back to bed. Queer! I can't fit it in.'

Mother and daughter looked at each other vaguely, as though trying to understand the situation. There was nothing they could do about it however, and in any case Sir Robert seemed pretty sure he had things under control.

'Inspector Hargraves ordered that neither of you are to go out this evening,' Sir Robert said presently, evidently deciding that his mysterious morning amnesia couldn't be explained. 'He was very specific about it.'

'Well, I'm not going out, anyway,' his wife answered, shrugging. 'And I certainly wouldn't with this horrible business threatening.'

'No hardship to me,' June commented. 'But I do wish the Yard would start showing results. It's not pleasant hanging under a cloud, and with a fresh threat on the horizon. Since Trudy's death the whole thing seems to be a nightmare — and no end in sight, either!'

'As for myself,' Sir Robert said, rising, 'I have very simple plans. I shall spend my time here in the lounge and catch up on reading various medical periodicals. Then, at eight forty five I shall have a bath, and then go to bed. I doubt if anybody would murder me in my bath,' he added dryly.

Maude suppressed a little shudder. 'And what about dinner? You're not giving yourself long after it before having a bath. Forty five minutes or so — As a medical man you should know that's a bit dangerous at your age.'

'I'm not having any dinner, Maude. As I've told you, I am not feeling too well. Maybe it will do me good to give my stomach a rest.'

And, his mind made up, Sir Robert clung rigidly to his plan. He did his best to ignore the Yard men as they remained in their positions, talking quietly to each other, reading newspapers and magazines, and generally trying to make themselves 'not there.' Protection duty was always tough at the best of times, even with a willing subject — and Sir Robert was anything but that, even though he did not say more.

According to plan he lost himself in reading until nearly eight o'clock, then as June and her mother departed for dinner he was left alone with the Yard men. They gratefully accepted the tea and sandwiches brought in for them, and so the watchdog business continued until at last Sir Robert threw down the medical magazine he was reading and got to his feet.

'Quarter past eight,' he commented, stretching and glancing at the clock.

'Yes, sir,' Sheard said respectfully, and for no reason at all checked the time with his wristwatch.

'Which brings me to another point.' The surgeon strolled across to where the two men were seated and stood looking down on them pensively. 'What happens when I decide to have my bath? Can't I have any privacy even for that?'

'I will check the bathroom over before you go in to bath, then afterwards I will guard the bathroom door, and Thompson here will watch the window from the outside.' Sheard seemed quite satisfied with his arrangements. 'I don't see how anything could happen under those circumstances.'

'No . . . ' Sir Robert reflected. 'Neither do I . . . Well, you'd better get busy. I want to get started.'

Sheard rose. 'Right, sir. Thompson will stay with you whilst I'm gone.'

The surgeon gave a rather rueful smile as the p.c. man strode actively from the lounge.

'The police are a nuisance in whatever capacity they appear,' Thompson commented. 'Sorry you have to be inconvenienced, sir.'

'You're only doing a job,' Sir Robert shrugged. 'If the rest of Scotland Yard were working half as efficiently as you I wouldn't grumble!'

Thompson said no more: he thought it

safest. Sir Robert prowled around the lounge for a while, plainly making a big effort to control his emotions, then he glanced up as Sheard came back actively.

'All's well, sir,' the p.c. man announced. 'Certainly nothing peculiar in the bathroom. You can go right ahead.'

'Thanks,' the surgeon said, rather dryly. 'I will join you again, gentlemen, when I have had my bath . . . Oh, you'd better guard my bedroom first. I shall disrobe there first, as I always do.'

Sheard glanced at Thompson. 'Hop outside,' he ordered. 'Keep a constant watch on the bathroom window until I tell you otherwise.'

Thompson went on his way, not particularly relishing the thought of a lonely vigil in the November night. Sir Robert hesitated a moment, glanced at the clock, and then began moving.

'I'll just tell my wife and daughter,' he said, and Sheard nodded as he followed behind him.

Now it lacked only thirty-five minutes to nine o'clock Sir Robert was having increasing difficulty in keeping himself under control, but he did manage to seem calm as he looked in the dining room.

'Going up to bath now, Maude,' he said quietly. 'Don't worry. Everything's under control, and the bathroom has been checked over before I even enter it.'

Neither June nor her mother said anything. They just couldn't. Sir Robert spared them the effort of words. He left the room and went quietly up the stairs with Sheard at a respectful distance behind him . . .

With a glance at his watch Sir Robert entered his bedroom and closed the door. Sheard came to a stop, lighted a cigarette, and propped himself against the wall. Even he was jumpy, and he was accustomed to assignments like this. Every moment he expected something to happen — but nothing did. He heard the sounds of Sir Robert disrobing within the room — then at last the surgeon reappeared, wrapped in his dressing gown and with heelless slippers on his feet.

'Everything all right?' he asked, rather tautly.

'Yes, sir.' Sheard glanced at his watch.

'Ten to nine. I shouldn't worry, sir. Everything's going to be all right.'

'Yes . . . I suppose so.'

The p.c. man looked surprised. 'You suppose so? Why do you say that, sir?'

'Damned if I know.' The surgeon pressed finger and thumb to his eyes. 'Just a sort of instinctive feeling . . . I suppose I've got nerves: that's the top and bottom of it — and probably a lingering cold too, which doesn't improve things.'

'Yes, sir. That'll be it.'

Sir Robert braced himself with a sudden effort and went on down the corridor to the bathroom. Entering it, he switched on the light and left the door open. Sheard stood on the threshold, looking in on the cased-in imitation marble bath, gleaming chrome taps, and delicate pastel walls.

'Watch until the last moment,' Sir Robert said, turning on the hot water and switching on the towel-airing rack. 'We can't do more than that.'

Sheard nodded and waited. The surgeon looked at the inset thermometer controlling the bathwater temperature and turned on the cold tap to reduce the heat. Then he gave a taut smile and came over to the door.

'Be with you later,' he said, and closed the door.

Sheard drifted to one side of the door and leaned against the post. Automatically he looked at his watch again — and it said five minutes to nine. Even his nerves were strained to the limit . . . He lighted another cigarette and listened to vague sounds within the bathroom.

Then presently even these sounds ceased. For a while, Sheard thought nothing of the quietness — then it dawned upon him that it should not be so. There ought to be the sound of splashing water — even perhaps singing in a fruity baritone. But there was nothing. Not the faintest suspicion of noise.

'Queer,' Sheard muttered, a premonition gripping him. 'Infernally queer.'

Down in the hall the big grandfather clock began to gong out nine solemn strokes, but long before they were finished Sheard had awakened to action. Turning, he thumped on the bathroom door.

'Sir Robert, you all right?' he shouted.

Still no sound. Sheard didn't wait any longer. He dropped his cigarette, stamped it under his heel, then took a running jump at the door. It creaked under the blow. The second time he was successful and with a numbed shoulder went floundering into the bathroom — to pull up short in amazed horror.

Over the edge of the bath Sir Robert's arm was dangling, a curiously tautened, strained arm it seemed, as though it were under enormous tension. Sheard looked at it incredulously and then crept forward.

Finally he had the full view. The surgeon, stark naked, was lying full length in the water, with just the one arm flung over the side. His very attitude was enough to satisfy Sheard. He had seen a man once in a similar position — in the galvanizing tautness of electricity.

Somehow Sir Robert had died, and violent electric shock was the cause . . . As the fact registered on Sheard's mind the hall clock ceased chiming below, and there were hurried footsteps coming up the stairs, obviously drawn by the noise of the shattering door.

4

Sawley Garson, scientific investigator, and one of the Yard's most brilliant backroom boys, was in the midst of chemical computations in his laboratory when Crowther, his man-of-all-work, looked in on him.

'Busy, boss?' he asked.

'Ever know a time when I'm not?' Garson growled. Then he glanced up at the wall clock. 'I know it's gone eleven so you can go to bed if you want to. Leave me some sandwiches. I may be working all night.'

'Yes, boss, but that isn't what I wanted. There's Inspector Hargraves of the Yard to see you. He apologizes for the lateness but says it's urgent.'

Garson sighed and tossed down his pencil. 'All right, show him in.'

In a moment Hargraves had entered. He did not find Garson particularly effusive, but then he seldom was. His sapphire blue eyes studied Hargraves keenly as he advanced across the laboratory.

'Hello, Hargraves.' Garson shook hands. 'Maybe it's the light, but I'd say you're fatter. Probably all the sitting down you do.'

'Knowing your elephantine sense of humor, I'll skip that,' Hargraves answered. 'I'm in need of help, and you're about the best man I can think of.'

Garson grinned, proffered his cigarette case, then scooped sandy hair away from his broad forehead.

'Who did what this time?' he inquired, when the cigarettes were lighted.

'This time it's murder,' Hargraves said quietly, finding a tall stool for himself. 'Three murders on the run — always with a warning beforehand, and in spite of police protection on two of them, they take place exactly as predicted. There's something uncanny about it. The third murder was tonight — electrocution.'

'The victim?' Garson asked.

'Sir Robert Dawson, the resident surgeon of St. Luke's Hospital.'

'So he got landed too,' Garson mused, and Hargraves looked at him quickly.

'Meaning what?'

'Meaning I've read the case in the papers — as I always do — and I've noted that Gerald and Trudy Dawson were murdered. The one with a car accident and the other with poison. Now Dawson himself has gone, has he?' Garson shrugged and considered his cigarette. 'Why should you want me? You haven't lost your touch in tracking down a murderer, surely?'

'Not when one exists, I haven't. In this case there does not seem to be one! That's why I want your help.'

'Doesn't seem to *be* one!' Garson repeated in amazement. 'Oh, come now!'

'Hear me out — and see what you think.' And in detail, as the scientist smoked pensively, Hargraves gave the facts. Not a single thing did he suppress. It would not have been to his advantage to do so.

'And tonight's business about capped the lot,' he concluded. 'That bathroom was thoroughly examined before Sir

Robert went to have his bath — and it was examined by a man in whom I have implicit faith. Yet the murder took place just the same. Sir Robert died of electrocution in his bath. I was called right away. We had to cut the power off at the mains before we dared touch him. I've got the electrical division working on the business now, trying to find out what happened. But even if they find the cause — as they will — I'm not much better off in so far that nobody strange has called at the Dawson home for many weeks, and certainly nobody had the chance to fix some kind of dirty work in the bathroom.'

'Not even anybody on the staff?' Garson asked.

'Most unlikely. There's only a maid — and not a frightfully bright one, either. Again, how did the murderer know that Sir Robert would have a bath at that time? Again, how was it nobody came in or out of the telephone box after warning him over the 'phone?'

Garson grinned and rubbed his acid-stained hands together.

'Very interesting,' he murmured. 'A

perfect exercise for the mind. Somebody is distinctly ingenious.'

'And I'm distinctly fogged!' Hargraves snapped. 'With this third murder I'm likely to get hauled over the coals by the Assistant Commissioner. Not unnaturally, he'll want to know what I'm doing — and he'll take a dim view of the fact that I haven't got anywhere! Frankly, I just don't know where to start.'

'I'm not surprised! But don't start getting the idea that these murders were committed by gremlins or fairies at the bottom of the garden. There's a killer all right, and one of the most ingenious ones we've yet come across.'

'Then you'll help me?' Hargraves asked, relieved.

'Sure I will. For one thing I like the fee the Yard pays me, and for another I've a yen for puzzles. I'll be on the job first thing in the morning, and then we can start at the bottom. Right?'

'Fair enough,' Hargraves assented, rising. 'By that time I'll have the electrician's report amongst other things, so you'll be able to have a look at it.'

Hargraves had very little sleep that night: he had too much on his mind; and he was back again at the office at 8.30 to study whatever information had come in. Quite a deal, as it happened. On his desk were photographs of the body in the death position; a medical report on the cause of death; and finally the electrician's findings.

Hargraves glanced at the photographs, noted briefly that death was due to electrocution — which fact he knew already — and then hurried on to the electrician's report. His brows down, he studied it carefully.

On removing the tile-work from round the bath side I discovered a wire had been soldered to the underneath side of the bath proper. I traced this wire back to the towel-airing rack, where it joined the main cable supplying the rack with power. This means that when the towel-rack was switched on — the power passing from one end of the towel bar to the other by means of a small element regulated by a transformer — there was also a direct current escape down the wire soldered to the bath. This had the effect of electrifying the metal base and side of the bath, and particularly the water within the bath itself. Death would occur the instant the victim touched the water, an effect completed by gripping the bath sides or coming in contact with it.

'I'll be damned,' Hargraves muttered, putting the report down slowly. 'When on earth was it done? Taking away the tile-work at the side of the bath, and putting it back to leave no sign, would be quite a job in itself. Then there would be the concealment of the death wire to the towel airer . . . '

He glanced up at a knock on the door. Without waiting for an answer Sawley Garson strolled in, his sandy hair looking even more disordered than usual.

''Morning,' he said genially. 'No objections to an early start, I suppose? I'm surprised to find you here, as a matter of fact.'

'I'm worried,' Hargraves said, rubbing his chin. 'The more I see of this Dawson

101

business the more baffled I get. Here, read this report from the electrician.'

Garson sat down and complied. When he had finished he lighted a cigarette and sat thinking.

'Well?' Hargraves asked irritably. 'What's your conclusion? How was that bath wired up?'

'I dunno. It just was — but we'll have to find out how. Anything else?'

'Just photos of the body and the surgeon's report.'

Garson picked up the photographs and studied them. After a moment or two he put them down again.

'Pretty obvious what happened. Sir Robert experimented first with one foot — a quite common habit — and instantly the electricity got him. He jolted forward under the shock, and fell in the bath, leaving one arm hanging out.'

'We know that,' Hargraves sighed, 'but when and how was the death wire fixed? Apparently nobody had a chance to do it, unless it was perhaps his daughter, wife, or the servants. And I'd stake my soul they wouldn't have the knowledge, and

Reserved for:

~~EYER~~

Collect by:

WINCHESTER

even less the wish.'

Garson thought for a moment, then: 'What about the chaps on guard? Can I have a word with them?'

'Sheard and Thompson — Yes, they might be here by now. I'm a bit early this morning. Even Sergeant Brice hasn't come yet. He never varies from nine o'clock.'

Hargraves switched on the intercom. 'Hargraves here. Send Sheard and Thompson in to me the moment they arrive — They are here now? Good! Send them along.'

In the space of a few moments the p.c. men entered, both of them looking sheepish. They felt keenly — and undeservedly — that laxness on their part had resulted in the death of Sir. Robert.

''Morning, boys,' Hargraves said. 'You know Mr. Garson?'

The two men nodded and waited. Garson himself took up the thread.

'You two lone wolves were given the job of watching Sir Robert on the day he died. What can you tell me — ? And don't start off by saying you've no idea how it was done. We don't expect you to have.'

'From the time we went on duty,' Sheard said stolidly, 'there was no stranger present. And none called — or indeed *had* called during the day. We were closer to Sir Robert than a shadow. When the time came for Sir Robert to take his bath I sent Thompson outside to keep a watch on the bathroom from the exterior, whilst I guarded the door on the landing. And I examined the bathroom before Sir Robert went into it.'

'But not the bath,' Hargraves remarked grimly.

'Well — no, sir. I never anticipated such a thing.'

'Of course you didn't,' Garson said genially. 'You're a p.c. policeman, Sheard — not a clairvoyant. Don't reproach yourself. You acted perfectly in accordance with normal rules.'

'Thank you, sir.' Sheard looked relieved.

'Now to something else . . . ' Garson hunched forward. 'What was Sir Robert's manner like? Did he seem bothered about the warning he had received?'

Sheard nodded. 'I think he was, but

being a man of the world he endeavored to treat it with contempt. Just the same I think the strain on his nerves was considerable.'

'Mmm. I won't ask you if you heard anything peculiar in the bathroom, because obviously you didn't. The murderer was far away at the time and, technically, Sir Robert killed himself. And you say nobody called at the house? Nobody who could have done the bath wiring under some pretext or other?'

'Nobody, sir.'

'For that matter,' Hargraves said, 'the wiring up could have been long ago. Only thing to do is trace every caller for weeks back.'

'You're slipping, Hargraves,' Garson grinned. 'Presumably other members of the family besides Sir Robert would take a bath regularly. They would also use a towel — and that means the electric towel-airer as well. Nothing happened to them — so we can narrow the field. The bath was wired sometime between Sir Robert taking his bath, and the one before him. We'd better follow that up.'

'Mmm — you're right,' Hargraves said. 'Frankly, I'm getting so tangled up with this business I can't see straight any more — '

'There's one thing I might mention,' Sheard said, pondering. 'Maybe it's nothing, and maybe something. In our business even a detail may mean something sometimes.'

'We're listening,' Hargraves said.

'Well, while Sir Robert was talking to his wife and daughter Thompson and I were present, of course — in the lounge. He was complaining that his memory wasn't all it ought to be, and that he didn't seem to know what he had done between ten and eleven in the morning.'

Garson leaned forward intently on the desk, his blue eyes sharp.

'His wife said he had been at home all day — but his daughter had something else to add. She said that around ten o'clock her father came down from resting and went into the garage. He spent five minutes in the garage and then went in the house again and up to the bathroom without explaining himself. He was in there quite a time, and then went to his bedroom and was not seen again until lunchtime . . . ' Sheard gave a shrug. 'That he went into the *bathroom* seems as though it might have some significance.'

'And he couldn't remember this particular incident?' Garson asked quickly.

'Apparently not, sir.'

Garson sat back and rubbed his acid-stained hands gently together. Hargraves looked at him and raised an eyebrow.

'Do you scent something there, Garson?' he inquired.

'I think so. Tell you later if it leads anywhere.' Garson looked at the p.c. men. 'Anything else?'

'No, sir. If I recall anything else I'll tell you.'

'All right, boys,' Hargraves said. 'You can go.'

The two turned and left the office, just as Sergeant Brice came in. He cast a sheepish glance at the clock and then at his superior and Garson.

'All right, don't worry,' Hargraves said.

'I know nine o' clock is your time, sergeant ... I'd better put you in the picture to date. You know Mr. Garson, of course?'

'Yes, sir. Morning, Mr. Garson ... ' And thereafter Brice listened attentively to what had gone before. At the end of it he stroked his jaw.

'Weighing everything up, sir, it sounds like suicide,' he said. 'To me, it looks as though there is some connection between Sir Robert visiting the garage and then the bathroom. Suppose, in that time, he wired up the bath?'

'I think he did,' Garson said calmly.

'You do?' Brice looked pleased. 'Then that bears me out, sir! He wired the bath up, so he could commit suicide.'

Garson smiled. 'But why did he choose such an elaborate and nerve-racking method? If you know your job you also know that suicides usually choose a comfortable means of exit — not a harrowing one. Again, how does that fit in with somebody ringing up and saying death would occur at nine o'clock?'

Brice considered. 'Well, perhaps Sir

Robert only said he got a message — Maybe he didn't really. That would explain the empty telephone box.'

'Come off it, man,' Hargraves growled. 'Larry Hayes and his boys heard the speaker, remember! There *was* a call.'

'Then that rips that to pieces,' Brice sighed; then he looked sharply at Garsen. 'But you said you think Sir Robert wired the bath!'

'I do think so — but I don't think it was suicide . . . I've a lot to check on first. And I think I'd better start doing it. Let me see now — To all intents and purposes it is triple murder. Gerald, Trudy and Sir Robert. First a car death; second, poison; and thirdly, electrocution . . . ' Garson gave a grim smile. 'Wonder what is planned for the fourth and fifth?'

Hargraves gave a start. 'Then you think as I do? That somebody is trying to exterminate the entire Dawson family?'

'On the face of things it looks very like it . . . First thing we'll do is check back on the Dawson place and see what they have to tell us. Besides that, we'll take a look at that bath. It interests me.'

Thereupon they went into action — and though he would not admit it openly Inspector Hargraves was a very troubled man. It was bad enough to still have the murder of Trudy hanging round his ears, and no solution. It was even worse to have the problem of her father's death added to it. Before long the Assistant Commissioner, to say nothing of the press, would be asking some very pointed questions as to the efficacy of Scotland Yard.

Both Mrs. Dawson and June were moody and quiet as Hargraves asked the questions. He did so as gently as possible, bearing in mind their bereavement, and Garson simply stood and absorbed everything, forming his own conclusions. He only came to life when the bathroom was examined, the door locked.

The tile-work still lay in a stack on the floor as the electrician had left it. Garson peered and poked, using his flashlight, and examined every detail, back to the towel-airer. When he had finished he rubbed a hand through his ginger hair.

'Rotten workmanship, but damned

effective for poor old Sir Robert,' he said.

'How do you mean — Rotten workmanship?' Hargraves asked.

'The actual wiring is the most amateurish job I've ever seen. The soldering of the wire to the underside of the bath is poor. There's a joint in the wire that isn't even covered with sticky tape. Nor is the joint to the main wire where the bath wire has been laced to it . . . Mmm, that reminds me of something.'

'What?'

'To make this connection to the main cable the power would have to be cut off. Let's see now . . . '

Without explaining himself further Garson marched off downstairs and tackled Lady Dawson. She listened unemotionally to all he had to say.

'To the best of my knowledge the electricity has never been cut off, Mr. Garson,' she replied.

'Since it probably happened between ten and eleven yesterday morning, in daylight, the loss of power would probably not be noticed. Do you mind if I have a look at the electric meters?'

'Help yourself,' Lady Dawson shrugged; then she added rather bitterly, 'I am hardly in a position to refuse you, even if I wanted.'

With that she led the way out into the hall, and to the big meter cupboard located near the front door. With his flashlight, Garson peered into the depths and then reflected.

'Electric cooker meter separate from the others,' he murmured to Hargraves, leaning over his shoulder. 'A cut of light and heating power wouldn't affect the cooker . . . Hmmm. Wonder if the maid knows anything?'

'We'll soon find out,' Hargraves said; and in a few moments Baines came tripping into view. She stood waiting, obviously with some nervousness, as Garson regarded her.

'Tell me something,' Garson said presently, with that easy good humor which was calculated to win the confidence of most people. 'Tell me, have you at anytime had reason to switch off the electric power here? I mean the main power as opposed to the cooker, which is a separate meter.'

'Yes, sir. I switched it off last night when it was getting dark — to look if a fuse had blown.'

Silence. Hargraves and Brice looked at one another, but from Garson's expression it was impossible to tell what he was thinking.

'To look for a fuse, you say? Why, had the lights gone out?'

'It wasn't that, sir: they wouldn't come on! When it was starting to grow dark I went to put the light on in the kitchen and nothing happened. I checked it with another bulb, and then I tried the hall light. Since none of them worked, I came to look for a fuse. To my surprise I found the main switch was off. When I put it on again everything was all right.'

'You just said you switched *off* last night to look for a fuse.'

Baines looked confused. 'I'm — I'm sorry. I should have said I *intended* to do. What I really did was switch on, since the lights and power were already off.'

'I see. You've no idea how this happened?'

'Not the slightest, sir.'

'How is the bath water heated?' Hargraves asked abruptly

'From the fire in the kitchen, sir. This house is a bit old-fashioned in some things — '

'I don't like immersion heaters, if that's what you mean,' Lady Dawson put in. 'Nor do I like electric heaters. I'm scared of electricity! Give me a gas or a coal fire every time.'

Garson reflected for a moment, then quietly closed the doors of the meter cupboard.

'Right,' he said to the maid. 'That's all. You can go.' Then when she had departed he looked at Mrs. Dawson. 'I think that's all we need here, madam — at least for the moment.'

'Well, what conclusion have you arrived at?' she asked sharply. 'I know you are not an official Scotland Yard man, Mr. Garson, so I feel I can say what I think. I'm sick and tired of endless probing and questioning and nothing to show for it! My daughter and husband have died at the hands of a murderer — of that Scotland Yard seems reasonably sure. And perhaps my son Gerald too. When are you going to get some results?'

'As soon as possible,' Garson answered blandly. 'We have to have every detail, of course. Naturally, nobody can be accused of murder until every fact is clear.'

'It seems to take such a time,' Lady Dawson sighed. 'I suppose, in the case of my husband, that once again it is a case of deferring the inquest until you have investigated the circumstances?'

'That's it,' Hargraves assented. 'I must apologize to you for all the questioning, madam, but we have our duty to do . . . We hope to have some satisfactory news before very long.'

There was little more to be said, and a few minutes later Hargraves, Brice, and Garson took their leave. They drove away from the house, stopped, and then held an impromptu conference.

'Well, what juice did you squeeze from that?' Hargraves asked.

'I might ask you the same question,' Garson shrugged. 'You're supposed to be a trained detective.'

Hargraves looked sour. 'Granted — but

that doesn't involve chasing a murderer — or murderess — who apparently doesn't exist!'

'He exists all right!' Garson's face was suddenly grim. 'And, mind you, I say 'he' loosely, since it might equally be a woman. Whichever sex it is, the killer is particularly clever, and completely ruthless. However, to go back to the Dawson home. The power and light was switched off and not put on again. I suppose Sir Robert himself did that. And I also suppose he did the bath wiring. It was plainly the work of an amateur, and I would put Sir Robert in that class. A man clever in surgery is not often a skilled electrician as well.'

Brice stroked his heavy chin. 'But if he switched the power off while he wired up the bath, why the hell didn't he put the power on again?'

'Because I fancy that once his job was done he quite forgot all about it — didn't even remember he had switched off the power. Remember, he said his mind was a blank during that period.'

'It smells to me like . . . hypnotism,'

116

Hargraves said slowly. 'Do you think that's possible?'

'Oh, it's possible,' Garson admitted. 'That angle had occurred to me in regard to Sir Robert, even if it doesn't quite explain the deaths of Gerald and Trudy. But you have something else to bear in mind in regard to hypnotism — namely that no person can be made to do anything injurious to himself under hypnotic control. The law of self-preservation is stronger than any hypnotist's will. Yet here we have a man preparing his own death! No, on first examination it doesn't stand up.'

'Pity,' Hargraves sighed. 'We have a hypnotist on tap whom we could question — Dr. Mason, the late Trudy's fiancé — '

'Yes, I know — the hypnotherapist. You told me last night in your long-winded report on things to date . . . Mmm. Let's see now — If Sir Robert knowingly — knowingly, mark you — planned his own death I maintain that he would not have planned such an unpleasant method. So that seems to suggest he planned his death without being conscious of it, at least during the period he wired the bath. The influence over him ceased at roughly eleven o'clock . . . And yet hypnotism doesn't answer it because you cannot will men or women to do injury to themselves.'

'Well, now where are we?'

Garson went on talking, half to himself. 'Trudy died from poison, which was straightforward. Gerald died from a motor smash that was somehow contrived to occur at the exact hour planned by the murderer. In fact, that applies in all three cases! And yet nobody ever came out of the 'phone box from which the call was made . . . It's a poser, all right.'

'Why not go back to the Dawson place and look for whatever was taken out of the garage?' Brice suggested. 'Apparently he didn't make a return trip, so whatever he took ought to be somewhere lying around. Probably in his bedroom.'

'Waste of time. We're pretty sure only Sir Robert could have done it. Where's the sense in gilding the lily?'

Silence, whilst Garson relapsed into a long spell of thought. He was interrupted finally by Hargraves.

'Something's bothering me,' he confessed at length. 'Why is it that this murderer, when he telephones, allows such a time lag between the first contact and the second? Further, why does the caller never give a chance for questions to be asked? He asks for somebody, leaves a long gap, then when they answer he makes a statement, once again after a long pause. I keep asking myself why? Doesn't sound natural.'

'There's nothing natural about this whole business,' Brice said gloomily.

'Have you any theory as to this gap in continuity of conversation?' Garson asked.

'Yes, but it's pretty preposterous. How about a tape recorder?'

Garson looked startled for a moment, and Brice's expression was frankly incredulous.

'Tape recorder,' Garson mused. 'Mmm, I wonder . . . You mean the murderer has already recorded his voice, allowed a gap for the time taken to get his victim on the 'phone, and then when he estimates that person will have answered he shoots off his warning? Naturally he can't answer questions, so he just makes a statement.'

'Sounds idiotic,' Hargraves confessed. 'But somehow I think there's something in it.'

'Don't see how there can be,' Brice commented. 'Even if a tape recorder were used, it would have to be got into the phone box, and somebody would have to start it and stop it, and then carry it away! Whichever way one looks at it, it's still impossible.'

'Well, it's a theory anyhow,' Hargraves insisted. 'What do you think of it, Garson?'

'Worth thinking about,' he responded. 'I've decided on a line of action. We've got to solve two things to begin with — First, how Gerald Dawson died; and second, who is there on our list likely to want to make Sir Robert and his family generally uncomfortable, even to the point of murdering them. The only way to get at that is to try and trace such a person through Lady Dawson. She might be able to help.'

Hargraves sighed. 'Somehow, I don't think so. I tackled Sir Robert himself on the matter of enemies, and he said he only had the enemies inseparable from his profession — such as those professionally jealous of him, and the other type, hating him for failure in operations and surgical matters. Every great surgeon must have those people who hate him if his skill happens to fail on certain occasions. Matter of fact, I think we can pinpoint that situation much more easily.'

'How?'

'Well, take the case of Trudy Dawson. She has a straightforward case. It was murder by poisoning, and that poison was administered by somebody. As I said recently to Brice, the answer lies in finding the poisoner. Get him, and I'll wager we have the killer on the other two occasions . . . It's an easier job than solving the electrified bath, or Gerald's mysterious car death.'

Garson nodded slowly. 'Mmm, maybe you're right — as far you yourself are concerned. I'm interested in the method, more than the murderer. Have you any direct idea of how to find Trudy's killer?'

'Uh-huh, the actor's party. You told me.'

'She was perfectly normal then. Since she was not in contact with strangers, except at the party, until the time she died I think maybe one of the party guests had the answer. I was going to begin the laborious job of questioning every one of them, then the rush of events didn't give me a chance. Now I'll go back to it and see what I can find.'

'Good idea,' Garson assented, even though he seemed to be thinking about something else. 'And you're leaving the theory about the tape recorder and the telephone kiosk alone?'

'Not by any means — but I can't do everything at once.'

'What you can do is leave Brice here to sort out and question the party guests whilst we follow up another line of search together. First — the spot where Gerald Dawson died wants very careful attention.'

'Why so interested in that? Isn't the empty telephone box more important?'

'Not *more* important — *as* important, but I prefer to begin with the first murder and work my way up. If we can establish a very material explanation for Gerald's death, we can also be sure — no matter how baffling it looks at first sight — that there's a simple explanation, too for the 'phone box. I suggest we drive down to the spot where Gerald died right away, and drop Brice at the Yard to sort out the party guest list.'

'Okay.' Hargraves gave a shrug, 'You seem to have taken the leadership in the matter, anyhow — which entirely suits me. But I'll warn you, there's nothing to be seen at the spot where Gerald died.'

'You've seen the spot yourself?'

'No — I've been sent the police reports and seen photographs. There isn't a thing that tells anything.'

Garson grinned and proffered his cigarette case. 'With all due respect to the police, Hargraves, they only see what they are trained to see. This time we're dealing with an off-the-track type of criminal who won't follow ordinary methods. That being so I shall proceed to look for the unexpected . . . Come on, let's go. Take full advantage of the daylight.'

5

By 11.30 — Sergeant Brice having been duly dropped at the Yard — the police car reached the spot on the deserted south coast road leading to Lessington, the spot where Gerald had met his death.

Hargraves put on the handbrake and then surveyed the landscape, afterwards comparing it with the photographs he had brought with him.

'Yes, this is the spot,' Hargraves said, as Garson glanced at him questioningly. 'The hill-track road at the eastern end of the South Downs. There's the waste land on our left in which Gerald's car crashed — and ahead's the bend in the road towards which he was traveling. If there's anything to see after all this time I'm a Chinaman.'

'How long ago will it be?'

'About six weeks.'

'Mmm. About six weeks of muggy weather, mostly damp, and no frost,'

Garson mused. 'Good conditions for our work. Not many imprints will have vanished.'

He opened the car door and stepped out onto the road. Then he stood looking at the road surface thoughtfully as Hargraves came to his side.

'Pretty bad road here,' Garson commented. 'You notice the macadam is in need of surfacing; it's smoother than a billiard ball, and, under greasy conditions and high speed, just made for skidding . . . In other words a perfect road on which to meet with an accident.'

Hargraves nodded. 'I don't think this road is used much by the general traffic because of its narrowness. It's a short cut to the main road to the coast.'

'And for some reason Gerald Dawson elected to use it on an October night under murky conditions. Just why, we don't know as yet. Now, let's see . . . '

Garson wandered to the road edge and stood looking at the uncultivated field bordering the road. It was at a much lower level and consisted of rank, winter-dry grass and here and there soggy, evil-looking pools.

'Traces of the car's track even yet,' Hargraves said, in some surprise. 'See here — Here's where he plunged over — and over there is where he ended up.'

Silently they studied two nearly obliterated dark tracks where brake-locked wheels leapt off the roadway into the field. Some twelve feet away in the field was a bare, churned-up patch.

'Well, where does that get us?' Hargraves asked at last. 'Since then there have been breakdown trucks, don't forget, to shift the damaged car. They'll have left tracks.'

'No doubt — but if they had any sense they'd enter the field by that distant gate there. They certainly wouldn't leap over this grass verge — too risky. What I'm trying to determine is *what* caused Gerald to take a flying leap to his death. From the look of these tire marks he braked fiercely, and then a skid developed and caused him to lunge into the field.'

'Only thing I can think of is a car approaching from the opposite direction,' Hargraves said.

'Anybody reported themselves as the driver of a car coming the opposite way?'

'No. Not a thing.'

Garson pondered something and then crossed the roadway and examined the smooth macadam carefully. At this point the road took a slow curve, ending presently in a complete bend. From the bend it curved upwards over the downs, following its deserted course to the sea.

'Tire skid-marks last many months if they're deep ones,' Garson said at last. 'Now, assume a car belting along here. The driver would come round the bend, and realizing that Gerald's car was going off the road he would automatically jam on his brakes. I say automatically: that is the reflex response of any motorist when he sees a possible crash ahead of him. Yet there are no marks of any tires. No skid-marks. Nothing. If it was an approaching car that caused the tragedy, the driver didn't pull up hard enough to leave the faintest trace.'

'Mmm,' Hargraves said, feeling that things were not getting anywhere.

'There has to be a *reason* . . . ' Garson

muttered. 'I'm trying to find it. Something caused Gerald to leap off the road, and somebody deliberately engineered it. We know that because he was warned beforehand . . . '

Garson started on another prowl, his eyes on the roadway. Hargraves followed him, mainly to show interest, not because he knew what he was looking for. He was just commencing to feel vaguely irritated by the whole business when suddenly Garson came a stop. He was standing at the rough, pebbly gravel at the side of the road. Hargraves looked too, but failed to notice anything.

After a moment Garson went down on his haunches and pointed to three small holes in the gravel, set in the design of a triangle. They were perhaps half an inch deep and had evidently only remained there because no traffic wheels would ever come so far over the edge of the road.

'Three holes,' Hargraves said at length, also squatting. 'What about it? They're not usual things to find at the edge of a road, I'll grant, but I'm damned if I can see their significance.'

'Let's take a guess,' Garson mused. 'The most likely cause of Gerald's accident was a blaze of light which prevented him seeing where he was going. A passing motorist might have dipped his lights to avoid trouble, and he would certainly have slowed up right away. In this case we have no traces of a motorist, but the dazzling light conception remains. I'll take a long chance and say that a photographic spotlight was used. Most of them will run from a twelve-volt car battery and the light they give is quite powerful on open focus — even more so coming suddenly in the darkness of the night.'

Hargraves raised his eyebrows. 'You're suggesting that somebody used a photographic spotlight out on the road here, connected to a car battery?'

'I am. These three holes in the gravel would be made by the tripod carrying the lamp. Since it's fairly heavy the indentations would naturally be pretty deep. Park the car some distance away and carry a long lead wire from the battery, then switch on when Gerald came tearing into sight. On a local road like this his was the only car likely, and it seems evident our murderer knew Gerald would come, as planned. Afterwards, fold everything away and silently depart, naturally leaving no skid marks; in fact no traces at all, except those three tripod holes from its spike-ended legs.'

Hargraves stood up and thought for a moment. 'The odd thing is that it's possible — and damned original, too.'

'It's not original, Hargraves. It's been used twice before in accident cases. And it's not odd, either. What else but the legs on a tripod accounts for three holes like this?'

Hargraves sighed. 'Can't think of anything — and even if you're right we're not much nearer. It doesn't necessarily mean a photographer did the dirty work. A spotlight is easy enough to get hold of.'

'We're going to accept it as a working theory,' Garson mused, strolling back towards the car. 'And it goes to prove that the killer is quite material and is using ingenious methods of destruction. The next thing we've got to do is work out the telephone kiosk mystery.'

Hargraves did not say anything. He was content to let the scientist handle things in his own way. So a return was made to London and, lunch over, the two set out for Belgrave Court and the puzzling telephone kiosk.

Once he was out of the car, Garson stood looking at the telephone kiosk thoughtfully, weighing it up. Not, so far as Hargraves could see, that there was anything unusual about the box. It looked normal enough and, as before, was in full service for anybody who wanted it.

'This,' Garson said, 'looks like being the real problem. Let's take a look.'

In a moment or two they had propped open the heavy door, then Garson stepped inside the kiosk and stood looking at the telephone set up. Everything was as it should be. Finally he lifted the instrument from its cradle and dialed the exchange.

'Number please?'

'Exchange? Are you receiving me clearly? No interference?'

'Who is that speaking, please?'

131

'Scotland Yard. Can you hear me?'

'Perfectly, sir,' the girl answered. 'No interference. Shall I call the supervisor?'

'No, no — everything's all right, thank you.'

Garson put the telephone back on its rest and looked about him. He traced the wires from the telephone itself, through the coin box, on the side, and up to the ceiling of the kiosk — then he went outside and studied the wires that traveled from the box to the underground telephone cables.

'A poser is right,' he said at last. 'At first sight I can't see how it was done.'

'You're licked then?' Hargraves asked disappointedly. Garson grinned.

'You know me better than that. There are many ways in which the trick could have been worked, but I want to look over a few telephone circuits I've got in my lab before I venture any opinion. In the meantime, I've no need to put this box out of action in order to study it. The post office might take a dim view of my wrecking their precious kiosk.'

'Up to you,' Hargraves said. 'If you

think it's really necessary to pull this box to bits I'll soon get the necessary authority.'

Garson shook his head. 'I'll work something out first . . . In the meantime have a constant watch kept on this kiosk.'

'I've got that already. Two patrol squad men keep it under constant surveillance, and they're relieved by two more men at night. There they are.'

He nodded to Elmington Crescent — the main road — on which a squad car stood. The two men inside were obviously watching intently but, having recognized Hargraves, were taking no action.

'They know what they're looking for, I suppose?' Garson asked, lighting a cigarette.

'Of course they do! They're watching for any suspicious looking character seen entering or leaving this box. They are watching for anybody who might tinker with the telephone inside the box, or behave in a strange manner.'

'Mmm. Mind if I have a word with them?'

Garson did not wait for an answer. He

strolled across to where the car was standing, and the patrol men inside saluted.

'Give whatever information Mr. Garson asks for,' Hargraves said, coming up.

'You've had this phone box under surveillance since yesterday, one or other of you?' Garson asked.

'Yes, sir. Nothing to report.'

'Has it been used at all?'

'Quite a few times, sir. Women chiefly, and one man. None of them did anything they shouldn't.'

Garson took a deep drag at his cigarette and pondered for a moment. Then he asked another question.

'Nobody's gone in or out with a small attaché case?'

The officer looked vaguely surprised. 'Why, no, Mr. Garson. Are we supposed to look for such a person?'

'Definitely yes. It might be of tremendous advantage. Keep your eyes open for such a person from now on.'

With that he nodded and moved to Hargraves' car. When they were within it Hargraves scratched the back of his head.

'What's the attaché case angle? I don't get it.'

'You ought to, after all that talk about tape recorders.'

The Chief-Inspector started. 'You mean — '

'I mean that the modern tape recorder is no larger than a small attaché case. It might even be concealed in the telephone box somewhere, only we haven't happened to discover where. Anybody leaving with one in a small case wants immediately questioning . . . However, that's in the future apparently. Let's get back to the Yard and see how the worthy sergeant's going on.'

Upon arriving back at the Whitehall office they found Brice in the midst of sorting out the list of party guests. He looked up quickly as Hargraves came in.

'Anything happened, sir?' he asked quickly. 'Any new development?'

'The marks of a tripod, and that's the lot,' Hargraves sighed, throwing his hat on the peg.

'Marks of a tripod, sir? How do you mean?'

'I'll explain later. It's a theory of Mr.

Garson's. How are you making out with that list?'

'Not bad. I'm noting the addresses down in the different areas, so that we can move in a more or less straight line without having to go back on our tracks. Incidentally, there's one thing that may be significant.'

'What's that?'

'There's a fellow here — a guest at the Warlock party that is — by the name of Jerome Kenton. And his address is 22 Porlock Avenue.'

'Well?' Hargraves asked. 'Ought I to be thrilled?'

'According to the map, sir,' Brice said, glancing at the district plan on the wall, 'Porlock Avenue overlooks Elmington Crescent, and incidentally the phone box which so interests us.'

'The devil it does!' Garson murmured, his eyes narrowing.

'That may be important,' Hargraves said, looking up. 'In fact we might begin our search right there.'

'If you take my advice,' Garson said, thinking, 'you won't do anything of the sort. Do you want to frighten the man off before you've even got started? I should skate round it, as carefully as you can . . . Anyway, that isn't my part of the job. I'm going home to work out this telephone box business. When I have something I'll give you a ring. 'Bye for now.'

On that Garson took his departure. Brice stood looking inquiringly at his superior.

'Get anywhere, sir?' he ventured again.

'Precisely nowhere. There's no explanation as yet for that telephone box — but maybe this discovery you've made about Jerome Kenton may get us somewhere. Might try Warlock and see if he can tell us anything.'

Hargraves reached to the telephone and in a moment or two had contacted Warlock at his hotel. In a matter of moments Hargraves had made his business clear.

'Jerome Kenton?' Warlock repeated. 'Why, yes, he's an old friend of mine. He's running a thought-transference fake on the halls.'

'A what?' Hargraves asked, frowning.

'A thought-transference fake. You know the kind of thing — mind reading. He says it's genuine, but I've got my doubts. Calls himself The Mental Marvel. He's on at the Royal this week in Hammersmith, along with his assistant, Maisie Grantham.'

'I see. And I presume that, as long as you've known him, he has always been doing this thought-reading business?'

'As a matter of fact he hasn't — that's why I don't think it's genuine. He used to be knife and axe thrower, with his wife as the target. He only stopped when he accidentally severely injured his wife. It broke him up completely.'

'How long ago was this?'

'About five years ago.'

'Mmm.' Hargraves made a note. 'I take it that Jerome Kenton is his real name?'

'Far as I know it is. I've never known him by any other name. Look, Inspector, you're surely not suspecting poor old Jerry of anything, are you? He wouldn't hurt a fly.'

'Unfortunately, Mr. Warlock, in my line

of business I am compelled to suspect everybody and everything until I've reason to doubt them no longer... Thanks for the information, anyway: it's been most helpful.'

'A pleasure, I'm sure.'

Hargraves put the telephone back on its rest and sat thinking for a moment, until he realized Brice was looking at him expectantly.

'Anything fresh, sir?' he asked, as Hargraves looked up.

The Chief-Inspector shrugged. 'Nothing much. Our friend who lives in a house overlooking the telephone box runs a mind reading act on the stage — presumably a faked one. Before that he was a knife-thrower. Make of that lot whatever you can.'

'Don't you think it would be a good idea if we went and had a chat with him?'

'Why?'

'Well — just to see what we can find out. After all, he is the only one on the list overlooking the — '

Brice paused, somewhat irritated, as there came a knock on the office door. A police officer entered.

'Miss June Dawson would like to see you, sir.'

Hargraves did not show the surprise he felt. He merely nodded, and a moment later June came in. She was looking vaguely anxious, and her usual air of pseudo-worldliness was entirely absent.

'I'm glad I found you in, inspector,' she said, as Hargraves shook hands and then drew up a chair for her. 'I've done something that wants stopping — if you think it necessary.'

'Oh?' Hargraves raised his brows. 'What have you done?'

'I've given an interview to a reporter from the *Argus*. He came this morning to ask for the background of daddy's life, so I told him everything I could think of. Dad was a pretty important man in the medical profession, you know . . . Afterwards, though, I got to wondering whether I should have done that or not.'

'I presume this was because of the report of his death?'

June nodded and waited, anxiety in her hazel eyes.

'Well, I can't see that it matters,' Hargraves said finally. 'I suppose a mention of your father's distinguished career is only to be expected. I only wish we could move a little faster in finding his murderer.'

'I mentioned that Scotland Yard hadn't had any success up to now,' June said, still in the same apologetic manner. 'After all, that's the truth, isn't it?'

'I'm afraid so.' Hargraves' expression did not betray what he was thinking. 'I think you can rest assured, Miss Dawson. You did not do anything wrong . . . Incidentally, why were you the one the reporter questioned? Wouldn't your Mother have been more appropriate?'

'Very probably, but she did not seem in the mood to wish to talk about father. I think the reporter sensed this, so he applied to me.'

'Mmm — quite understandable.'

June got to her feet. 'Well, that's all I came for, inspector. Unless there are any questions you wish to ask me?'

'No, I don't think so. We're proceeding as rapidly as we can, and I expect developments very shortly. That's all I can say at the moment.'

June nodded and moved towards the door. 'And in the meantime I suppose there'll be an inquest on father?'

'Not in this case. It will be adjourned, as in the case of your sister, until we have completed our investigation. The funeral arrangements can proceed.'

June nodded somberly, but did not say anything. Hargraves shook her hand and slowly closed the office door behind her. Then he glanced across at Brice.

'Been more to the point if she'd kept her mouth shut,' he said, rather bitterly. 'Concerning the Yard, I mean. When the Assistant Commissioner reads that bit about the Yard having had no success up to now he's going to hit the ceiling. Three murders and no definite action. I'm not risking it . . . '

He lifted the telephone, dialed the well-known number of the *Argus*, and, in a few moments was speaking to the city editor.

'Hargraves here,' the inspector explained. 'I want you to do some special editing for me, Dick. I believe one of your boys has been interviewing Miss June Dawson about the life story of her father.'

'Oh, has he?' The city editor seemed surprised. 'Which one was it? Do you know?'

'I haven't a clue — but Miss Dawson told me the story she told him — and it strikes me some deletions are necessary.' Hargraves frowned to himself. 'Wait a moment, Dick! None of your boys would go out on an assignment like that, surely, unless you yourself had authorized it.'

'Just what I'm thinking. Wait a moment whilst I check up.'

The telephone clanked at the other end as the city editor put it down. Thereafter Hargraves waited through several minutes, meantime pursuing a variety of troubling thoughts. Then the city editor's voice came back.

'You there, Hargraves? I think you must have your facts mixed up somewhere. Nobody on my staff has been to interview Miss Dawson — or even thought of it. Sure you've got the right paper?'

'Yes — quite sure,' Hargraves answered

slowly. 'All right, Dick, thank you. I'll worry about it from here on.'

Hargraves replaced the telephone slowly and gave Brice a grim look. The sergeant scratched his bullet head.

'I don't get it, sir. Why should Miss Dawson say she was interviewed when she wasn't?'

'I believe she was — and she accepted it as a perfectly normal interview. The fortunate part about it is that she decided to tell me. That reporter — so called — didn't want a story. He wanted *June*, but for what reason? That's the problem.'

They were silent for a moment; then Hargraves shrugged. 'On the face of it there isn't much we can do. We can only act when we see what happens. In the meantime I think we'd better start the eliminating process from the list of Warlock's guests — beginning with Jerome Kenton. Up to now he seems the most likely person. Let's go: we might catch him in.'

No further time was wasted. Brice did the driving to Porlock Avenue and, as the map had shown, it completely overlooked the expanse of Elmington Crescent, with the baffling telephone kiosk plainly in sight — and empty at the moment. Further away, on the main road, the police squad car was visible, ever watchful.

Number 22 Porlock Avenue overlooked Elmington Crescent at right angles, and was one of those massive Georgian residences in which central London abounds. In response to Hargraves' vigorous ringing of the old-fashioned bell-push a buxom woman of perhaps fifty came to the door.

'Good afternoon, madam.' Hargraves raised his hat politely. 'I believe a Mr. Jerome Kenton lives here?'

'Yes, that's right. He's one of my boarders. I take in quite a lot of theatricals, you know.'

'Is he in at the moment?'

'Yes. You can go up to him if you like. Third door on the first landing, at the front of the house.'

Hargraves nodded and led the way up the stairs. Since both he and Brice were in plain clothes their official capacity was not betrayed — and the high hedge of the front garden was concealing the police car — but the landlady was entitled to her suspicions, and probably had them too.

'Front of the house, sir,' Brice murmured, as they went along the first landing. 'Faces the telephone box. Worth noting.'

'Uh-huh,' Hargraves agreed, and then tapped lightly on the third door.

There was a sound of movement from within and abruptly the door jerked open to reveal a smallish man with a wide forehead, dark untidy hair, and extraordinary light-colored eyes. In the poor afternoon light filtering onto the landing they seemed to be a colorless gray.

'Well?' he asked unsociably, in an unusually heavy bass voice.

'Mr. Jerome Kenton?' Hargraves asked, and as the man nodded Hargraves displayed his warrant-card. 'We're police Officers, Mr. Kenton. We'd like a word with you.'

'I haven't much choice, have I? All right, come in. I can't think what you can want with me.'

Kenton preceded the pair into a fairly roomy combined bed- and sitting-room. Hargraves settled down in the single armchair, which faced the window. It gave a view across to Elmington Crescent and the telephone box. Brice sat near the table with his notebook surreptitiously placed on his knee. Kenton stood in front of the low fire and his pale eyes aimed questions.

'Nothing serious about this visit, Mr. Kenton,' Hargraves said. 'Just a matter of routine questioning. For your information, a young lady by the name of Trudy Dawson died recently in peculiar circumstances. We believe she died because of poison . . . I believe you were at a party recently, given by David Warlock?'

'Correct.' Kenton hesitated for a moment, then a slow look of horrified amazement spread over his lean features. 'Did you say Trudy Dawson? Why, she was at the party!'

'Exactly.' Hargraves gave a grim nod. 'Don't you read the papers, Mr. Kenton? You'd have known about her death if you had.'

'I glance through them. I never was a

great reader . . . But about Trudy: what do you want to know?'

'I'm checking up on everybody who was at that party — yourself included. Have you ever had any associations with Miss Dawson, outside of that party?'

'None at all,' Kenton replied promptly. 'I met her there, thought her a very charming girl, and that's all there is to it. The news of her death is a big shock.'

'Yes, I suppose it is.' Hargraves thought for a while, his eyes on the distant, empty telephone box through the window. Then suddenly Kenton gave a little exclamation to himself.

'You'll excuse me a moment, gentlemen?' Kenton asked. 'I have the gas burner in the next room here — some cooking I was doing.'

'Of course,' Hargraves said; then when Kenton presently reappeared he asked, 'I understand you are a mind reader, Mr. Kenton?'

'Well, sort of,' Kenton smiled. 'It gets a fairly good living on the halls, anyway. I claim I'm a genuine mind reader, but I can't find many people who'll believe me.'

'You're at the Theatre Royal, I believe?'

'For a short season,' Kenton acknowledged. 'With my partner, Maisie Grantham.'

Hargraves nodded slowly. 'And before that you used to be a knife thrower?'

Kenton frowned. 'You seem remarkably conversant with my stage career, inspector.'

'Simply a matter of having all the facts about the people I visit,' Hargraves shrugged. 'Am I right about the knife-throwing?'

'Entirely,' Kenton assented. 'I only gave it up because my heart wasn't in it after the death of my wife. I made a mistake in the act — a knife landed dangerously close to my wife's heart. She was rushed to hospital, but she couldn't be saved.'

'I see,' Hargraves said quietly. 'You have my sympathy, Mr. Kenton — though probably you have got over the tragedy by now. Tell me, since I'm not very well up in these things, was your knife-throwing act genuine? I always thought the knives were faked by means of traps springing at the point where the knives ought to appear — suddenly flashing them into view whilst the real knife was skillfully put out of sight.'

'It can be done that way by sleight-of-hand, and often is,' Kenton admitted. 'In which case there is no danger to the subject. But in my case it was genuine. I threw the knives — and I did it for years without mishap. Then on that one occasion I slipped up. How, I don't know. It cost my wife her life, and me my sanity, pretty nearly. The whole business was called 'Death from Misadventure.' I never threw a knife again.'

Hargraves got to his feet. 'Well, thank you, Mr. Kenton, for being so explicit — and I'm sorry I had to trouble you about this business of Trudy Dawson . . . Oh, by the way. Have you always had the same name as now? Was it ever different, for stage purposes?'

'No. I've always been Jerome Kenton. On the halls I'm known now as the 'Mental Marvel,' but that's just a tag line.'

'I understand. Incidentally, at this party of David Warlock's you met Dr. Mason, I presume? The late Trudy's fiancé?'

'Yes. I met him.'

'I should imagine you are a keen judge of character, Mr. Kenton: you would almost *have* to be in your present business. What was your opinion of him?'

The pale eyes looked questioning. 'Is this for the records, inspector, or are you asking me off the cuff?'

'It's not for the records. I'd just like to know for my own satisfaction.'

'All right, then. I didn't like him — not one little bit. I believe he's a hypnotherapist by profession, but how anybody could trust themselves to him is beyond me. I am very sensitive to mind reactions, inspector, and I sensed a cruelty and hardness in his make-up that definitely repelled me . . . Purely personal opinion, of course, but since you asked me there it is.'

'I see.' Hargraves mused for a moment and then turned to the door. 'Well, thanks very much, Mr. Kenton. I won't take up any more of your time. If you're ready, sergeant?'

Brice nodded and accompanied his superior out of the room and outside once more to the car. They looked at each

151

other when they were seated.

'Why all those questions about Dr. Mason, sir?' Brice asked. 'Is he important enough to warrant them?'

Hargraves shrugged. 'Not at the moment, but I might as well have the reaction of an outsider — which, I might add, does not in the least coincide with my own. I rather liked Mason, what I saw of him, and at the present moment I don't intend to hold anything against him, not in my personal thinking, anyhow.'

'And Kenton? What was your opinion of him?'

'It's rather hard to say. I had chiefly a negative reaction: I neither liked or disliked him, He seems to be telling the truth, and he's a typical pro doing his best to make a moderate living. Seems fairly clear he took it on the chin when his wife died.'

'So I thought. Doesn't seem much we can do about him, does there? And I suppose it's just coincidence that his room happens to overlook the telephone box in question?'

'Seems that way. We — '

Hargraves broke off as the short wave radio to headquarters suddenly came to life. He listened to the intoning voice in the speaker.

'Urgent call for Chief-Inspector Hargraves. Reply if receiving me. Urgent call for — '

Hargraves picked up the mike. 'Okay. Go ahead. Hargraves speaking. Over.'

'You're asked to telephone Miss June Dawson right away, inspector. She said she has important news for you. Over.'

'I'll attend to it. Over and out.' Hargraves switched off — then he checked Brice as he was about to switch on the ignition. 'We'll not wait until we get back to the office,' he said. 'This must be extremely urgent, otherwise June would never ring me. I can take it from our mystery box on the corner.'

Brice nodded promptly and followed Hargraves out of the car. In a moment or two they had crossed to the box and the inspector dialed the Dawson number after consulting his notebook. The voice of Baines, the maid, floated over the wire.

'Inspector Hargraves here,' the inspector said quickly. 'I believe Miss June

153

wants a word with me?'

'Oh yes, inspector. I'll tell her. Just a moment.' Hargraves waited, looking meanwhile about the telephone box as though he hoped some clue would present itself. Nothing did. Then the girl's voice reached him, obviously agitated.

'Hello, Inspector. I've been trying to get you for some time. About twenty minutes ago I received a warning on the 'phone.'

Hargraves started. 'Another of those telephone warnings, you mean? Naming an hour?'

'Yes. Just the same as Trudy and dad received. The time was given as nine tonight . . . Inspector, I'm scared! I really am! What am I to do?'

'A moment. Let's get this clear. You received the warning twenty minutes ago. You're sure of that?'

'Quite sure. I'm looking at my watch at the moment. Yes, it was twenty minutes ago. Baines answered it first. I took up the 'phone; then after a fair interval that voice spoke. It used just the same words, and everything.'

'Just try to keep calm, Miss Dawson,' Hargraves said urgently. 'Stay exactly where you are and I'll be over to see you. You promise me that?'

'Yes, yes. I promise.'

'Right. Now ring off and wait for me coming.' Hargraves put the 'phone back on its cradle, then went outside the box to tell the waiting Brice the news. Brice's eyebrows went up.

'You don't mean she got the warning from *this* 'phone, sir?'

'That I don't know yet. I surely hope not, else I'll be sure we're chasing a ghost. Quick — back to the car.'

The moment they had reached it Hargraves switched the radio into action and spoke rapidly.

'Hargraves speaking. Contact Mr. Hayes, chief post office engineer, and tell him to come to my office immediately if he can. I'm on my way there now. Over.'

'Mr. Hayes is here at the moment, sir — asking if you can be contacted. Over.'

'He is? Good! Put him on the radio immediately. Over.'

'Hello Hargraves,' came the engineer's

voice after a moment. 'I wanted to tell you, personally, that the Dawson 'phone line has been in action again . . . Over.'

'Yes, so I believe,' Hargraves responded. 'I've just been on to Miss Dawson myself. Another warning, I understand. What I want to know from you is: did it come from the same telephone box as before? Over.'

'The very same,' Hayes replied immediately. 'If you've got men outside that box they ought to have seen somebody, otherwise I'll begin to think, with you, that the 'phone kiosk is haunted. Over.'

'Definitely it must be!' Hargraves' voice was bitter. 'I've had reason to watch that damned box nearly all afternoon, and not a living soul's gone in or out of it . . . Okay, Larry, thanks for the information. I'll be seeing you. Off.'

Hargraves switched off and compressed his lips. Brice gave a baffled glance.

'It's impossible, sir!' he declared finally. 'It just couldn't happen!'

'I think the same — yet according to the evidence it *has* happened . . . All right, so we're up against a phantom, or something very like it. I'm going on to see June, but I want support with me. Stop at the Yard on the way and I'll contact Garson and try and get him to come with us.'

6

Sawley Garson was in Hargraves' office within fifteen minutes of being telephoned, and he listened in complete silence to the tale the harassed inspector had to tell. At the end of it he gave his wide, schoolboy grin.

'Knocks quite a lot of things on the head, doesn't it?' he asked dryly.

'Definitely it does,' Hargraves retorted. 'And I don't see anything to grin about, Garson! I had Jerome Kenton in line as a possible suspect — but now that's blown sky high. I was talking to him at the very time June Dawson was getting her warning.'

'And you saw the telephone box and it was empty at the time the warning was received?'

'Yes . . . I just said so.'

'All right, don't bite my head off.'

'Sorry,' Hargraves apologized, sighing. 'This case has got me so tied up I hardly know what I'm doing any more . . . Anyway, let's get things in focus. Did you dope out anything on that telephone circuit you were going to figure out?'

'Uh-huh. I've worked out how a telephone can be made to ring without any of the usual gadgets being used. By 'gadgets' I mean lifting the telephone from its rest, dialing the required number, and so on. You can telephone anybody, anywhere, without resorting to any of these methods.'

'No wonder the 'phone company complains their profits are down,' Brice commented.

'But to do it,' Garson added, 'you have to have a pretty good knowledge of telephones, and the circuit on which they operate.'

'Even so,' Hargraves said, 'and granting a 'phone call can be made without recourse to the usual methods, there must still *be* somebody in the box to make the call, surely?'

'Not necessarily,' Garson shrugged. Then after thinking for a moment he asked, 'Have you the time now to listen to an explanation, or do you want to get out to June Dawson's?'

Hargraves glanced at his watch. 'Should be safe to wait a bit longer. Let's have it.'

Garson nodded and pulled a pencil from his pocket. Then on a sheet of paper he began to draw a design of the inside of a telephone box. When he had finished, everything was there. The phone itself, the rest, the money box, the buttons for communication or money back, the junction box, fuse box, and main conduit for carrying the wires to the box's exterior.

'It's simple enough,' he said. 'In fact anybody could do it if they studied the intimate details of telephone construction and circuit. We have a wire here — ' He indicated the spot with his pencil — 'which, when you dial, automatically sets up contact with the number you require. Now, the Dawson line is a four-number line. Take four separate wires and solder them to the four numbers you want — behind the dialing disk I mean — and then send a small electric current through them, and you get the same effect as if you dialed. The number is contacted, and the 'phone at the other end rings. Naturally, these four wires are hidden inside the 'phone and can't be seen from outside. Clear so far?'

'Fair enough,' Hargraves agreed. 'And then what?'

'I want you to imagine a tape recorder — here . . . ' And Garson placed the point of his pencil on the main fuse box. 'I want you to imagine it behind this aluminium plate, completely out of sight. From its output point a wire runs to the output of the telephone. On the tape is a recorded voice. Automatically, the vibrations of the voice — the *vibrations*, mark you, and not the actual sound — are transferred to the telephone wire without needing to use the telephone itself, since the transfer is direct to the wire . . . Are you still with me?'

Hargraves, who had been looking interested, suddenly seemed unconvinced.

'Can't be done, Garson! You'd never get a tape recorder in that fuse box. Even the smallest of them is miles bigger than that box.'

'Here's one that isn't,' the scientist

grinned, and from his capacious overcoat pocket he pulled out an object no larger than a good-sized matchbox. Hargraves and Brice stared at it in fascinated interest. They stared even more when, snapping back the small lid, Garson indicated minute tape reels and tiny buttons no larger than pin heads.

'Where the devil did you get that?' Hargraves demanded at length.

'*Get* it? Dammit, man, I *made* it! Over a year ago. And what one man can make, so can another. This tape recorder is one of the smallest there is, yet it reproduces perfectly. Naturally, the secret is in transistor valves of extreme smallness, and everything else correspondingly reduced. Playback can be amplified to any strength by a separate amplifier.'

'Hmm.' There was a bothered look on the inspector's face. 'Mighty neat piece of work, Garson, and I'll grant you that one that size would fit in a telephone junction box — or fuse box. But you'd still need somebody to stop and start it.'

'This one, yes,' Garson agreed. 'But I don't think you need anybody to start the one we're looking for. I could even modify this one so that it would be operative by remote control.'

'How?' Brice asked interestedly.

'By putting in a radio unit — which would make remote control possible over a distance by a separate radio unit.'

'You mean,' Hargraves said slowly, 'like those automatic lawn mowers? You sit in the chair with a 'gadget' and it operates the mower's radio motor — which in turn makes the mower cut the grass?'

'All in the house that Jack built,' Brice added. 'If it comes to that anything can be controlled by radio if need be.'

Garson's face became suddenly grim as he looked at the inspector intently.

'What I'm suggesting, Hargraves is this: Our murderer is a good scientist with a fair knowledge of radio. He has a small transistor-valve recorder placed in the 'phone box, arranged to operate by radio control. It automatically rings the bell wires once it starts up, probably by a device moving over electrical pointers, each pointer being connected by wire to the four separate wires which constitute the Dawson number — behind the dialing disk that is. The tape starts up, asks for somebody, then pauses to allow time for the somebody to appear — or rather speak — at the other end. When the message is given — the exact time of its duration being known to the operator — his remote control apparatus shuts the instrument off. Perfect! Nobody in the phone box, and no sign of a recorder, either.'

'Suppose somebody entered the box and tried to get a number whilst this thing was operating? What then?'

'They'd be unlucky. They'd get a blank — not even an 'engaged' tone. 'That's one of the chances our murderer is taking, and so far it's come off all right. Most people would just assume a technical fault and try another box.'

'Then,' Hargraves said slowly, 'you mean that warnings have been recorded in one strip on the magnetic tape? One for Gerald, one for Trudy, one for Sir Robert, and now one for June? In the same voice?'

'Exactly. Maybe there's even a fifth one

for Lady Dawson, if it's the murderer's intention to wipe her out too.'

Hargraves lighted a cigarette absently and dragged at it for a moment. Garson put the minute recorder back in his pocket.

'Look in the telephone kiosk, and I fancy you'll find a recorder in the fuse box,' he said. 'If not there, then the junction box. I'm not the official police, but if you want my advice I should have the job done immediately.'

'And if we find the recorder and remove it, the culprit will know we're not far behind him,' Brice remarked. 'Is it a good idea to give the enemy such advance notice?'

Garson shrugged. 'All right — just look if the thing's there and satisfy that much of your curiosity. It's not my business, after all.'

'We'll look all right,' Hargraves said, 'Preferably at night when our movements won't be seen.'

'Seen?' Garson looked surprised.

'I'm thinking of Jerome Kenton. From his room across the square he could study every detail of our movements. By night we'd be quite safe. In fact doubly so, because in the evenings he's giving his stage show at the Theatre Royal.'

'Then you're back to believing Kenton may be the culprit?' Garson asked.

'I'm not entirely sure, but he ranks high on the list. Because of that — in spite of what you said — I decided to interview him, as I told you when you first arrived.'

'I don't think he *can* be our man, sir,' Brice put in. 'For one thing, June Dawson got her warning at the very time we were with Kenton — and he certainly didn't fiddle around with any remote control radio apparatus whilst we were with him. How, then, did the recorder start up to give the message? Equally, how did it stop when the message was finished? And there's another thing — Kenton has a heavy bass voice — I might even say a real gravel pitch — and yet the voice that speaks to the victims, or intended victims, is smooth and soft. It doesn't match up.'

'It might, if Kenton got somebody else to do the talking for him,' Hargraves mused; at which Garson gave a grim chuckle.

'You know better than that, Hargraves. The criminal who'll share the secret of murder with a second person hasn't yet been born. No — it's too damned risky. If Kenton is our man, then he created the warning voice some other way, *not* by bringing somebody else into it. You can take that as certain.'

'His voice and the warning voice could not be more different,' Hargraves insisted. 'I've heard the warning voice over the post office engineering recorder and I know what it's like. I'm wondering if, in spite of the general rule that a murderer does not share his secret, Kenton may not have been forced to use a second party. David Warlock, the actor, for instance. His voice could easily suit the warning tones, or at any rate he could make it do so.'

'That,' said Brice, 'still wouldn't explain the recorder starting and stopping whilst we were interviewing Kenton. He looks like a dead lead to me, sir.'

Silence. Then Hargraves crushed out

his cigarette impatiently and got to his feet.

'This damned business is like a nightmare!' he complained. 'It isn't the sort of thing any normal policeman should have to investigate! Just what are we chasing — a phantom?'

'You're chasing somebody who's remarkably clever, but still of the earthly variety,' Garson shrugged. 'Somebody who knows that modern science, properly applied, can make rings round you down-to-earth policemen. He's a product of the modern age, this killer of yours.'

'Why does he take the trouble to warn everybody before he kills them?' Hargraves demanded. 'Answer me that!'

'Ego, Hargraves, pure and simple. There never was a criminal born who didn't have ego highly developed. Have a look at what Hans Gross has to say about that. It's one of the failings that help to leg a criminal down. In this case the murderer says death is due at such an hour — and in spite of everything you've done so far it has always come about. Result — one wide grin of triumph on the face of the murderer and the feeling that he is not as other men. He is a controller of destiny and the arbiter of life and death. There is no real *need* for the warnings, that I can see anyway, therefore we have to accept the conclusion that they are intended to baffle the police and satisfy the ego of the perpetrator . . . Which reminds me, we'd better be getting to June Dawson hadn't we?'

'Did you say 'we'?'

'I did. So far, if you'll forgive me, you haven't made much of a job of saving the threatened victims. I'd like to have a shot myself. Even if I fail I might learn something interesting.'

'Okay,' Hargraves grunted. 'Come if you want. Later on we'll have a look at that telephone box when it's properly dark.'

Garson nodded and rose to his feet; then a thought seemed to strike him.

'Wait — Did you say the post office engineers had made a recording of the voice speaking on the Dawson line?'

'Right,' Hargraves said, reaching for his hat and coat. 'What about it?'

'Just for my own satisfaction I'd like the tape for my own use. I'd rather enjoy listening to it in my lab.'

'Simple enough,' Hargraves said, crossing to the intercom. 'Do you want it sent to your home?'

'Yes. Crowther will be there to receive it.'

Hargraves gave the necessary instructions over the intercom, switched off, then turned purposefully to the door.

'Let's go. We can grab a drink of tea and some sandwiches and then carry on to the Dawson home, and let's hope that this time we can avert a further tragedy.'

* * *

When eventually the three men arrived at the Dawson residence in the early evening they found a restive, pale-faced girl anxiously awaiting them. Baines showed them into the lounge, where both June and her mother were seated before a blazing fire — but the girl rose instantly and hurried across the big room.

'Thank heaven you've come, Inspector

Hargraves. I've been like a cat on hot bricks ever since I got that message. Mother and I had even got to wondering if you were coming.'

Hargraves smiled faintly. 'I gave you my promise, Miss Dawson — and here I am. Good evening, Lady Dawson,' he added, to the surgeon's widow as she sat watching.

Her own greeting limited itself to a nod — even when Sawley Garson was introduced. Hargraves, knowing full well what Lady Dawson thought about Scotland Yard, cleared his throat.

'I thought it would be as well if I came myself on this occasion,' he said, seating himself. 'And Mr. Garson also decided he would be personally present.'

'I can't imagine why,' Lady Dawson said bitterly. 'Recalling Mr. Garson's investigations into the light and power of this household I cannot see that he can help much.'

'Everything leads to a definite conclusion, madam,' Garson himself said blandly. 'I can understand your acerbity towards the police in view of what's happened. But this time we are trying to make it certain that nothing tragic will happen.'

Lady Dawson tightened her lips and said nothing. After a moment she resumed her fixed staring into the fire. Silently, June slid down into her former armchair and looked at Hargraves hopefully. Gone was all her air of phony worldliness. She looked just like a frightened little girl, nor was she apparently deriving much comfort from her mother, either.

'What am I to do at nine o'clock, inspector?' she asked urgently. 'Tell me — so I shan't be likely to do any of the things Trudy and my father did.'

Hargraves asked: 'What exactly had you *intended* doing?'

'I've no fixed plan. I thought that if I sat tight in here and had guards all round me, I might escape trouble . . . But it is for you to say.'

'That would seem to be your best course,' Hargraves said, after thinking for a moment. 'You agree with that, Garson?'

'Entirely,' the scientist said — but he seemed to be thinking of something else.

'You had better make it clear to me, gentlemen, whether you expect a meal,' Lady Dawson said. 'Both June and I have abandoned the idea of a normal dinner in the evening: it seems rather purposeless with only two of us, and so much trouble hanging over our heads. However, if you wish — '

'No need at all,' Hargraves interrupted. 'In fact I think it would be a good idea to remain in this room and have Baines bring refreshment in the form of sand-wiches, or something.'

'As you wish.' Lady Dawson's manner was still cold. 'I take it you think there is less danger in this room than elsewhere in the house?'

Hargraves shrugged. 'Not particularly. There's danger everywhere, if it comes to that, but it's easier to handle it when it's localized . . . We intend to stay here until nine o'clock, after which time I don't think there'll be any more trouble.'

'As you wish,' June said quietly, struggling hard to appear at ease. 'I'm completely in your hands, inspector.'

Garson, who had been musing to himself next to Sergeant Brice, suddenly seemed to come to life. He looked across at June intently.

'It occurs to me, Miss Dawson, the answers to a few questions might help things. I believe you had, or gave, an interview with a reporter from the *Argus* this morning? So Inspector Hargraves tells me.'

'That's right, Mr. Garson.' June looked at Hargraves. 'Did I do anything wrong, inspector? I did tell you about it.'

'I know. But the queer part is that no reporter ever came from the *Argus*. I checked up on it.'

Both June and her mother started, then glanced at each other.

'But — but he did!' Lady Dawson insisted. 'I was even asked if I would give the interview. I didn't feel up to it, so I left it to June.'

'There are one or two points in regard to that interview that I'd like to get straight,' Garson said slowly. 'That is, if you have no objections, Hargraves?'

'None whatever. Carry on.'

'Right . . . Tell me something, Miss Dawson. What did this fellow from the *Argus* look like?'

'Oh, medium height, blond hair, and I think he had dark blue or dark brown eyes. I couldn't quite tell because of thick-lensed spectacles.

'Hmmm . . . ' Garson glanced at Hargraves' rather crestfallen face. 'Does that match up with our friend in Porlock Avenue, inspector?'

'Couldn't be less like him,' Hargraves sighed, at which June looked sharply from one to the other.

'What do you mean? Have you been trying to identify this man from the *Argus* with somebody else?'

'Something like that,' Hargraves admitted. 'Don't let it worry you. There's an answer to everything. Let's try something else. How did he speak, this reporter?'

'Very nicely. I'd say he had a rounded, masculine voice.'

'Deep?' Hargraves put in quickly.

'Fairly. Pleasantly baritone.'

'Would you call it an unusual voice?'

Garson questioned

'Not really. I've heard plenty of men who talk like that. Herby Mason, for one — poor Trudy's fiancé. Or maybe it's his professional manner that makes him that way. I suppose a hypnotherapist *has* to have a nice voice.'

Hargraves took out his notebook and looked at it. It listed Herbert Mason as tall, black haired, and genial within the limits of his professional capacity. Certainly it did not ring a bell in connection with a medium sized, blond haired man from the *Argus*.

'Anything else?' Lady Dawson asked rather abruptly, in the sudden silence that had descended.

'Yes, I think there is,' Garson said slowly. 'How have you *felt*, Miss Dawson, since this man from the *Argus* departed?'

'Felt?' June looked astonished. 'How do you mean? Ought I to feel any different? You don't suppose he made an emotional impact upon me, do you? Just sitting there — where you are now, as a matter of fact — asking questions.'

'Where I am now,' the scientist

repeated slowly. 'Mmm — in the daylight I would have my back to the light . . . Where did you sit, Miss Dawson?'

'Here — facing him. In this armchair.'

'Did he seem quite normal when he talked to you?'

June was commencing to look amazed. 'Of course! Isn't this getting rather ridiculous?'

'Perhaps,' Garson admitted absently. Then he relaxed. 'I just wanted to satisfy myself about something.'

Lady Dawson rose to her feet in obvious impatience and pressed the bell-push.

'I'll order refreshment, gentlemen,' she said curtly. 'Perhaps it may help to clear your minds . . . '

* * *

When the refreshment had been disposed of it was half past six, and about the comfortable lounge with its blazing fire there hung an air of pleasant homeliness — but it was limited to the surroundings and was no part of either June or her mother. Both of them were plainly suffering from nerves, despite the attempt they were making to control themselves. Not that Hargraves or Brice were particularly relaxed either: they sensed strongly the responsibility that was upon them. Perhaps the least disturbed was Garson — deep in the armchair, smoking interminable cigarettes, and gazing full fathom five into the dancing flames of the fire.

Presently conversation resumed, and it was Hargraves who started it. He did not once refer to the matter on hand, but adopted every commonplace topic he could think of, from the weather to qualifications of Tibetan mystics. Most of the time June tried to give intelligent answers. She smoked as she talked; but finally, towards half-past eight she could hold out no longer and became suddenly silent.

Hargraves ceased talking and looked at Garson. The scientist peered back at him through a blue haze of cigarette smoke. Lady Dawson shifted uneasily and glanced at the mantle clock.

'Gentlemen,' she said pointedly, 'there is not very long to nine o'clock. Do you still think there are no last minute preparations you ought to make? I confess I am disappointed! All of you have just sat here — and done nothing.'

Garson aimed sapphire blue eyes at her. 'On the contrary, madam, thinking can accomplish a great deal more than physical activity sometimes. As for preparations, there are none to make. The next move is up to your daughter.'

'Up to me!' June exclaimed, surprised. 'How do you make that out?'

Garson shrugged. 'It's fairly easy. Your father died through his own actions when he stepped into the bath. I see no reason why you shouldn't make a move to bring about your own destruction . . . The difference will be that you will be prevented. So, I'm waiting to see what you intend doing.'

'I don't intend doing *anything*! I'm just going to sit tight. And you're forgetting something! My sister Trudy didn't die through any action of her own: she was poisoned. How do you know *I'm* not?'

'Simply because you have none of the symptoms. If I had been here when your sister died I think I could have stopped it. I would have recognized what was the matter. However, anybody can be wise after the event ... I've been watching you more closely than you realize during this evening, Miss Dawson. Every move and every reaction. Now I'm waiting to see what you do as nine o'clock approaches.'

'I never heard a more cold-blooded approach to a problem!' Lady Dawson protested. 'What you are saying, in effect, is that you expect my daughter to do herself some kind of injury that will result in her death ... Why *should* she?'

'Because I think she will be unable to help herself,' Garson replied grimly. 'We'll find out soon enough.'

Hargraves scratched the back of his head, completely at a loss. Not that Sergeant Brice looked any the more knowledgeable ... As for June, she gave an irritated look and then relaxed in the chair, her fingers working agitatedly.

Eight forty-five. Garson lighted another

cigarette and never took his eyes from June. For another ten minutes she fought for control over her nerves, then apparently they got the better of her. She jumped to her feet and glanced at the clock, which needed only five minutes to nine.

'For heavens sake why can't we *do* something?' she demanded, looking at each in turn. 'This quietness is too much for anybody to stand in my state of mind . . . Let's have the television on, or something.'

She strode actively towards the corner and reached towards it; then she looked up in surprise as she beheld Garson, his hand gripping her arm tightly.

'Leave that television alone, Miss Dawson,' he said quietly.

'Don't be absurd! I *want* it! Let go of me!'

June made a sudden savage effort and almost twisted free of Garson's grip — but not quite. Fiercely though she struggled — a struggle indeed that seemed beyond all reason — she was forced further and further away from the television and finally pushed back into the armchair.

Only then did she break down. Her hands flashed suddenly to her face and she broke into convulsive weeping. Grim-faced and silent Garson looked down at her.

'For heavens' sake, June, don't be so ridiculous!' her mother exclaimed, coming across to her. 'All this fuss because you've been prevented from having the television. You might be a child of two!'

'Reaction, Lady Dawson,' Garson said, glancing at her. 'She'll be all right in a moment. Don't be too hard on her — '

He glanced up as the clock struck nine; then he turned to the vaguely bewildered Hargraves.

'I think we've a good answer to all this in the television, Hargraves. Let's have a look.'

He crossed quickly to the set and, puzzled though they were, Hargraves and Brice quickly followed him. They stood watching as Garson unplugged the set from the mains and proceeded to examine it. When at last he had taken the back off he gave a grim smile.

'Very pretty! Very pretty!' he said, indicating the interior. 'Wire connected from the mains supply to the on-off switch. If June had turned on that switch she'd have had enough current to fry her! There's even copper wire threaded through the on-off switch to make certain. See? And I don't need to emphasize that a television set carries a very high voltage.'

'What are you saying?' Lady Dawson asked incredulously, coming across.

'I'm saying, madam, that if your daughter had switched this set on she would have been electrocuted,' Garson replied grimly. Then he wrenched out the offending additional wire and handed it over. 'There you are. A short length of copper wire, the dividing line between life and death.'

June, who seemed to have recovered somewhat, rose slowly from her chair. She held her forehead as though it ached.

'Mr. Garson . . . ' She moved slowly across towards him. Do you mean that *I* was going to switch on this television set?'

All save Garson stared at her in amazement. He alone seemed to be expecting the girl's remark.

'Yes, you were,' he answered, putting an arm about the girl's shoulders. 'And if I hadn't forced you into that chair there you'd have done it, too. You don't remember it, I suppose?'

'It may sound silly, but I don't. I don't remember anything since we were arguing about mystics in Tibet . . . ' June gave a little shudder and then glanced up at the clock. Her face began to brighten. 'It's past nine o'clock, Mr. Garson! It's past nine! And nothing has happened.'

'And it won't — for the moment,' Garson told her, leading her back to the chair. 'Sit down, Miss Dawson, and try and pull yourself together. Maybe a little brandy would help,' he added, to her mother.

Lady Dawson promptly supplied it from the sideboard and then stood waiting whilst Garson reconnected the television to the power plug, and then came thoughtfully across to the center of the room.

'What the devil's it all about?' Hargraves demanded. 'Who fixed that wire in the television?'

'Unless I'm greatly mistaken, it was June herself,' the scientist answered, and at that the girl lowered her glass in amazement.

'*I* did?'

'Yes. Just the same as your father took on the more complicated job of wiring the bath which killed him. In other words, you both acted under orders.'

'Whose orders?' Lady Dawson demanded. 'You're not making sense, Mr. Garson.'

'Maybe not, but then this isn't a case which lends itself to clear-cut explanations — at least not yet.' He settled once more in the armchair and looked at June intently. 'Somewhere after the time when that supposed reporter from the *Argus* visited you, you put that extra wire in the television, Miss Dawson. You won't have any knowledge of doing it, but you may recall — as your father did — a blank in the sequence of your normal life. Today, after the *Argus* man left you, there must be some period you can't account for.

Think — and think hard.'

June frowned as she finished the remainder of her brandy. Then at length something seemed to dawn upon her.

'I remember the *Argus* man going, Mr. Garson, because I saw him to the front door — but somehow I don't remember what I did after that. At least not until lunch time, and that part is perfectly clear . . . It would seem as though about half an hour is missing which I can't account for.'

Garson nodded slowly. 'Time enough to wire the television, anyhow.' He looked across at Lady Dawson. 'Where were you in the time prior to lunch, madam?'

'Resting in my bedroom. That's why I didn't want to be bothered with the reporter. In fact I told him I was going upstairs to rest for awhile.'

'Which gave him a clear field to work in,' the scientist mused. 'Yes, it fits. You could do the job on the television without anybody watching you.'

June nodded slowly, waiting for the next.

'He evidently made a snap decision and

took a chance that nobody *but* you would switch on the television before nine o'clock. Considering the way you'd be watching for something to happen — and listening too — it was a quite logical inference on his part. You'd hardly watch television when expecting something dreadful to happen to you. Yes, it all fits in.'

'Are you saying,' Lady Dawson asked slowly, 'that this bogus reporter from the *Argus* was the murderer of my husband, daughter, and probably son? The potential murderer of June?'

'I am,' Garson nodded. 'And the method — in the case of your husband, son, and June here — had it come off in her case — was post-hypnotism.'

Hargraves gave a start. 'Now wait a minute, Garson! I had that idea myself a while back, and you squashed it. You explained to me the logic of the fact that nobody under hypnotism can be made to kill themselves because of the stronger impulse of self-preservation.'

'True — but I didn't say that a hypnotized person couldn't fix up all the details concerned with his own — or her own — death without actually killing themselves. That *can* be done. Under hypnotism you can be made to rig up a scaffold for yourself, but self-preservation will prevent you taking your own life.'

Hargraves rubbed his chin and looked doubtful. Garson gave him a rather tolerant smile.

'Don't flog your brains to pieces, Hargraves. I'll explain in full later on. This is hardly the time or the place . . .' Getting to his feet he looked down on June and her mother. 'Try not to worry, ladies,' he said quietly. 'For the first time the killer has failed, and we're beginning to get his measure. In your particular case, June, you were hypnotized by the bogus *Argus* reporter — almost certainly without your realizing it. He gave you two post-hypnotic orders, operative when he had left you. The first was to wire the television, for which he'd give you full directions that you couldn't possibly forget. The other was to switch on the television at nine o'clock. You obeyed the first one, but not the other because I stopped you . . . Understand?'

'I understand,' June shivered a little. 'It's horrifying to think anybody could have such malign power.'

Garson shrugged. 'Hypnotism is a science, the same as psychology, psychiatry, and kindred mental arts. Surely you've seen cases where a person is ordered by a stage hypnotist to do certain things under the influence of, for example, certain music? They always do it to that particular piece of music as long as the influence lasts. That's a harmless example of hypnotism. This other sort is cruelty incarnate. Complete sadism.'

'And what do you suppose will happen now?' Hargraves asked.

Garson reflected. 'For the moment I think everything will be safe. For one thing, the murderer won't know for a while yet that his attempt on June has failed, and for another we may have nabbed him before he can do anything further. I'd suggest you have a couple of men come from the Yard, inspector, and keep a guard on this place. We'll be busy elsewhere . . . You ladies can relax,' he added, glancing at them. 'But remember this, Miss Dawson: don't go out, or have contact with any outsider until you are told it is safe to do so. Right?'

'I promise,' June said seriously.

'Right! Then we'll get back to the Yard, Hargraves, when you have those two p.c. men to take over. Get busy on the 'phone.'

7

With the two plain clothes men duly installed, Hargraves, Brice, and Garson returned to the Yard, arriving in the inspector's office towards 10.15. Immediately he sent a phone call to the canteen for supper for three to be sent up. Only then did he relax and look at Garson questioningly.

'Well, Garson?' he asked. 'How about that more elaborate explanation you promised me?'

'And you shall have it,' the scientist smiled. 'June's case shows that it is hypnotism we're fighting, even as you suspected at first. Naturally the person responsible for the hypnotizing knows he can't force his victims to take their own lives — but he *can* implant in their minds a task they must do at a certain time, and doubtless he has implanted the necessary instructions as well. With Sir Robert it was the job of wiring up the bath from the towel airer. With June it was the task of wiring the television. We'll leave Trudy and Gerald out of it for the moment . . .

'Now, having ordered them to do these jobs at a certain time he gave a post-hypnotic order for yet another instruction to be obeyed. With Sir Robert it was the order to take a bath at nine o'clock and with June the order to switch on the television at nine, in the way we saw. Notice that neither of the secondary orders have any suggestion of danger, and all knowledge of previous tasks performed, whilst under hypnotism, have vanished. So, Sir Robert obeyed his second order — and died. June obeyed, and we saved her. But in neither case was there any suggestion to the victims that murder was intended, therefore the resistance of self-preservation did not need to operate. Understand?'

'Entirely,' Hargraves agreed. 'And it's about the most devilish hypnotic persuasion I ever heard of . . . But what about Trudy and Gerald. What happened in their cases?'

Garson reflected. 'From what you've

told me, I don't think any hypnotism was used in relation to Trudy. It was a straight forward poisoning murder, with the killer knowing that it would take until about nine o'clock for the poison to work . . . However, Gerald suggests hypnotism again, in so far that he suddenly decided to journey along a certain road, and reached a certain point at a certain time — namely nine o'clock. In other words, the hypnotist knew this would happen, and prepared death accordingly.'

Hargraves was silent as tea and sandwiches were brought in. Then as he munched a sandwich he made an observation:

'It makes you wonder why there aren't more murders of this kind.'

'The mental side of things is way outside the sphere of most people,' Garson shrugged. 'And certainly there are few criminals who practice it: they haven't the intelligence. For that reason the police don't encounter it very much. Any that do occur are probably not detected and are relegated instead to the 'Death from Misadventure' category.'

Garson took his cup of tea and began to drink pensively. Hargraves picked up another sandwich and chewed slowly.

'I'd sooner have the crack-on-the-head with an ax kind of murder than this ultra-refined business. Gives you the feeling you're dealing with something that isn't really there ... All right, we've established the method,' he said finally. 'So what happens now? We look for the hypnotist?'

'Obviously,' the scientist said. 'But that isn't going to be easy. The man from the *Argus* — supposedly — is the man we want, but who is he? The only likely people on our list are Dr. Herbert Mason, who is a hypnotherapist and able to get at poisons; and Jerome Kenton who, as far as we know, is not a hypnotist at all. Just a knife-thrower turned thought-reader.'

'But,' Hargraves said, 'he claims his mind-reading is genuine. If he can really read minds — and there are many who think it possible — he ought to be able to practice hypnotism, or at least have a good idea of the technique.'

'An interesting point,' Garson agreed.

'But there's also the problem of motive. What *is* the motive? A crime without motive has no logic. Still further, who owns the mystery voice which speaks on the telephone?'

'And without definite proof we can make no arrest . . . ' Hargraves gave a sigh. 'All right, we've got to have the definite proof, but where the hell to start! That's the problem.'

'First,' Garson said, rising actively, 'I think we ought to examine that 'phone box and see if there's any sign of the tape recorder. Soon as you're ready we'll go.'

'Right now,' Hargraves said, getting to his feet. 'Come on, Harry,' he added to Brice. 'This is one of the times when we shan't get much sleep, I'm afraid.'

The sergeant merely shrugged and accompanied the two men through the building to their waiting car outside. Afterwards, they soon covered the distance to Elmington Crescent in the sparse night traffic. They pulled up behind the squad car carrying the two night duty men, and in a moment or two Hargraves was questioning them.

'Anybody been round that 'phone box?' he asked.

'Only an old woman, sir,' the man at the wheel answered. 'She took some time over her call — and then came out.'

'You didn't question her, then?'

The patrol man looked surprised. 'I didn't see any reason to, sir. She was a perfectly harmless old lady — '

'And she's been the only one to use that box?'

'All we've seen, sir. It was about an hour ago when she was here.'

Hargraves glanced at his watch. 'In other words, around ten o'clock? All right. Keep watching.'

Somewhat grim-faced, Hargraves straightened up and gave Garson a glance.

'I don't like it,' the inspector said. 'I have the feeling that we may not find what we're looking for after all.'

Garson did not say anything, but he led the way swiftly towards the telephone kiosk. Once within he quickly unscrewed the fuse box and then compressed his lips as he found nothing inside it. Next he tried the junction box, and got the same answer. There just was nowhere else the tape recorder could be hidden, except perhaps the money-box. This he quickly unscrewed and peered into the recess. There was nothing there that shouldn't be.

'Well, that's that!' Hargraves said bitterly. 'Some use leaving men on guard! They ignored an 'innocent old woman,' and I'll bet my boots it was the man we want. If I wanted to stretch it further I'd say it was Jerome Kenton, finished with his theater act. He could easily hide a transistor tape recorder under the skirt he'd be wearing. Damn!'

'I shouldn't worry too much,' Garson said, lighting a cigarette against the piercing wind.

'You haven't got an Assistant Commissioner to answer to!'

'Even if I had I still wouldn't worry. It seems to me that this happening has rather strengthened your case, instead of weakened it.'

'Strengthened it?' Hargraves repeated in amazement.

'Certainly. It nearly points a direct sign

to Jerome Kenton. This afternoon you visited him. For the first time he realized that the police were looking into things. Tonight, at the first chance, he moves away the recorder he undoubtedly had in this box. Clear cut evidence, surely?'

'Maybe . . . ' Hargraves looked across at the night-shrouded house in Porlock Avenue. 'It's a thousand pities I haven't got a search warrant. I'd examine number twenty-two from top to bottom!'

'We can soon get one,' Brice put in, and Garson gave a rather cynical chuckle.

'Some good it would do you. If Kenton *is* our man he'll have moved all traces of incriminating evidence by this time. You shouldn't have given him warning, Hargraves: but it seems it's no use talking to some people!'

'I did what I thought was necessary!' Hargraves snapped, controlling his temper with difficulty.

'We're dead set on Kenton apparently,' Brice said, 'but how do we fit him in with the *Argus* reporter? And according to your reasoning, Mr. Garson, that reporter chap was the hypnotist we want.'

'No doubt of it,' the scientist said.

'A man might assume many disguises, and even change his voice,' Hargraves mused, 'but he certainly couldn't alter the color of his eyes. The reporter's were dark blue or brown, according to Miss Dawson, yet Kenton's are a kind of watery gray or blue. Kenton has dark hair and the reporter was blond. Only thing that checks is the height . . . I just don't know what to think.'

'Since that's the case,' Garson said, 'you'd better pursue some other trail until you're absolutely sure of your man. In the meantime I'll do the same thing. I'm going back home right now to study the tape from the post office engineers, granting they've sent it, of course. I'll be in touch with you again when I've something relevant to report.'

'Fair enough,' Hargraves shrugged, obviously disconsolate. 'We'll give you a lift as far as the Yard. You left your car there, didn't you?'

'Right!'

★　★　★

Whilst Hargraves and Brice went home to get some sleep — and, as far as Hargraves was concerned, perhaps some new light or angle on the problem — the tireless Garson prepared himself for an all night session with his scientific instruments. He arrived home to find that the post office tape had been duly delivered, after which he told Crowther to retire and then took himself off to the laboratory. Thereafter, to the usual accompaniment of strong cigarettes, he set himself to examine the tape recording with scientific instruments, making constant notes meanwhile.

And at the Dawson residence, all was quiet. June and her mother retired in the normal way, and even if they did not sleep comfortably they at least were not disturbed by any evidences of danger. For the two p.c. men guarding the grounds, it was a tedious, seemingly never ending vigil.

The least comfortable was Hargraves. Practically all night he was mentally exploring that which had already happened, and seeking new approaches to the problem. Only when he got to the office at nine the following day had a line of exploration opened to him.

'It seems to me, Harry,' he told the sergeant, as he came in a few minutes after him, 'that it would be easier if we could find the motive behind all this. Given that, we could probably decide on the person responsible.'

'Yes, sir,' Brice agreed, rather woodenly.

'There are not many motives in the world,' Hargraves resumed. 'They all boil down to certain basic factors like money, jealousy, hatred, and revenge. Money we can eliminate because it doesn't fit. Jealousy? No, that doesn't work either. Our murderer doesn't seem as though he need be jealous of anybody — '

'Unless we think of Dr. Mason,' Brice interrupted, pondering.

'Why him?'

'Well, he's in the same hospital as Dawson, isn't he? Or rather Dawson *was* there until he was murdered. Did Mason perhaps resent Mason's position and wanted him out of the way?'

'No, you're off beat there.' Hargraves shook his head. 'For one thing, Mason

201

could hardly be jealous of Dawson. They have different lines of business so to speak — or did have. Mason's field is exclusively hypnotherapy. Dawson, on the other hand, was a surgeon. Again, why should Mason want to kill his potential father-in-law, fiancée, and maybe Gerald too? It doesn't ring a bell at all . . . Besides, we're back on the problem of the bogus *Argus* reporter, whom we feel sure is the genuine killer. He was a medium sized man. Mason is a tall one.'

Brice shrugged. 'All right, sir, I'm beaten there. Sorry.'

'No need to be sorry. All suggestions are helpful, even if they are wrong. Now let's see what else we have . . . Hatred? Of what? Doesn't seem to tie up when the whole family is involved. I should say revenge fits more adequately. Revenge on the entire Dawson family for something they have done in the past. One or other of them responsible for some act or other, and the whole family is being made to pay in retaliation . . . Now where are we?'

'Probably something Gerald did,' Brice

grunted. 'He seems to have been a pretty doubtful quantity — and he was the first to be murdered, remember. Maybe he did wrong by some girl and her father, or brother, or somebody, is taking revenge.'

Hargraves did not say anything immediately. He seemed to be pondering deeply over what Brice had said, from which fact the sergeant took heart . . . Then suddenly Hargraves slapped his hand down on the desk.

'Wait a minute! I believe I've got something! Jerome Kenton's wife!'

Brice stared, disarmed by the fact that his own theory had not even been mentioned.

'His wife?' he repeated. 'What about her?'

'Dammit, man, you know the facts,' Hargraves said irritably. 'She was seriously injured in a knife-throwing act. Remember what Kenton said? She was rushed to hospital, but couldn't be saved.'

'Well?'

'Which hospital was it, I wonder? Which surgeon tried to save her? Kenton didn't say anything about a surgeon, but it's quite obvious that the woman wouldn't be left to die. An operation of some sort was probably performed, but she didn't survive it. After that, as Kenton said, his sanity nearly went. Look back on the notes you made of his conversation and corroborate me.'

Brice picked up his notebook and studied it; then presently he nodded.

'Yes, you've got it correct, sir . . . And the more one thinks of it it's certainly an angle, even if Kenton doesn't match the bogus reporter from the *Argus*.'

'I'm not bothering about that for the moment: there may be an explanation somewhere. Now let's see: we don't know which hospital Kenton's wife was rushed to, but there's one sure way to find out. Study the newspapers and find out when the accident happened, and exactly where. We can soon locate the nearest hospital to the spot. He said five years ago, didn't he?'

Brice searched his notebook again. 'He didn't say, sir. But I have a note here to the effect that Mr. Warlock put it at five years ago, when you telephoned him.'

'Oh, yes — Warlock! I'd forgotten about him . . . All right, let's spend a morning with the newspapers, Harry, and see what we can dig out.'

Already feeling better now he had a definite line of action to pursue, Hargraves grabbed his hat and coat and led the way out of the office. Together they walked to the *Argus* building further along the Embankment. Hargraves' reason for choosing there was two-fold: for one reason it was a national daily covering anything of interest throughout the country, and for another the editorial staff were renowned for their friendly cooperation with Scotland Yard. They had never been known to refuse any reasonable request . . . nor did they do so on this occasion.

Hargraves' request for the files of the newspapers for five years ago was immediately granted, and thereafter he and Brice sat in a quiet reading room, browsing through paper after paper and yawning with the very boredom of it. It was two hours later and close on lunchtime when Hargraves suddenly alerted and stabbed his finger at a column.

'Here we are, Harry! Take a look at this!'

The sergeant immediately abandoned his own search and came over to where his superior was sitting. He read eagerly a short announcement that had the head-lines: KNIFE THROWER'S WIFE INJURED. The column said briefly:

Last night at the Rialto Theater during a knife-throwing performance, injury was sustained by 'Venus' — the lady on the receiving end of a series of nine knives. The thrower was Jerome Kenton, and the target his wife Elaine, otherwise known as 'Venus.' She suffered severe injury near the heart and was immediately rushed to St. Luke's Hospital, where despite an emergency operation she afterwards died.

'That's it!' Brice exclaimed, his eyes bright. 'Jerome Kenton himself, and it was his wife. And she finished up in St.

Luke's, where Sir Robert was the resident surgeon for a number of years. Ten to one he did the emergency operation.'

'Yes — very possible.' Hargraves was thoughtful as he closed up the file. 'I don't know the answer to lots of things, Harry, but it seems to me we've got a clue to work on at last. Let's get some lunch and then we'll check up on St. Luke's.'

This they duly did, arriving at St. Luke's just before two o'clock, where Hargraves immediately made contact with the resident surgeon succeeding Sir Robert Dawson.

'I can find you the case history of Mrs. Kenton if you wish,' the resident surgeon said, when Hargraves had explained the circumstances.

'I'd be glad of it, doctor. Thanks very much.'

The doctor departed from the ante-room, to return presently with a bulky file. He set it down on the table, consulted the alphabetical index, and then thumbed through the leaves. Finally he turned up the relevant entry.

'Here you are, inspector! Mrs Kenton

was admitted to this hospital with a serious chest injury. An emergency operation was performed — Er, do you want the medical details?'

'No, no,' Hargraves said, listening. 'Just read on, please.'

'The operation was not successful. The surgeon concerned was Sir Robert Dawson, resident house-surgeon at that time. He was given a knighthood a year later, you know,' the doctor added gravely, looking over his glasses. 'Clever man, Dawson. We shall certainly miss him.'

'I'm sure,' Hargraves said, rather brusquely. 'Anyway, thank you for the information you've given: it covers everything I wanted to know. I'm most grateful.'

'Not at all. Only too glad to help.'

With that, Hargraves and Brice took their departure in a thoughtful mood. Outside in the car they glanced at each other.

'It begins to make sense, sir,' Brice said. 'Our killer seems to have been Kenton after all, despite the many things that are yet unsolved. Motive: revenge for the death of his wife at the hands of Sir Robert. Just the same, I'll swear it was not Sir Robert's fault. He wouldn't willingly kill Mrs. Kenton, surely?'

'Obviously not. Even surgeons make mistakes, but plainly Kenton has got hold of the wrong idea and thinks it was negligence. That may tie up with him nearly losing his reason. Probably he's still a bit unbalanced, but that aberration would not prevent him working out a murder plan with diabolical efficiency. So, as far as we can see now, he's taking revenge on the whole Dawson family.'

'What do we do then? Go and arrest him?'

Hargraves sighed. 'No. We haven't got any proof. We have many theories, and every suspicion points towards Kenton — but he can still shelter under that damnable evasion known as 'the reasonable doubt.' I don't have to tell you that a man may be caught with a knife in his hand, and even the dead body at his feet, yet he can't be arrested — even less convicted — without irrefutable proof.

And that we haven't *got*. At least, not yet.'

'Well, do we really need to have that?' Brice argued. 'It seems to me we've got enough to arrest him in any case — on suspicion.'

'Have we?' Hargraves raised an eyebrow. 'We'll need more than that to satisfy the Assistant Commissioner, my lad. First, we don't know yet *how* the killings were committed: we suspect hypnosis but we haven't proof of it. We have even less proof when we remember that the actual hypnotist — as exemplified by the man from the *Argus* — bears no resemblance to Kenton. Secondly, there's the case of Trudy being poisoned. How and when did Kenton administer the poison?'

'At the David Warlock party. That's obvious.'

'It's *not* obvious, Harry: it's just a very reasonable assumption; the same as the assumption that Kenton planted a transistor tape recorder in the telephone box. But where is the recorder now? We have no trace of it. Again, where does the 'different' hypnotic voice come from, which doesn't resemble Kenton's in the least? Lastly, how and when did Sir Robert and Gerald come to meet up with the hypnotist in order to *be* hypnotized? All these points have got to be cleared before we get a direct line pointing to our man . . . For the moment we can only suspect Kenton. We can't arrest him until we know beyond a shadow of a doubt.'

'We've established motive, anyway,' Brice said. 'That's something to go on. What do we do next?'

Hargraves said slowly, 'As Garson pointed out, it is very unlikely that Kenton will have any incriminating evidence in his rooms by now, otherwise I'd get a search warrant and look. It would also give away the fact that we're on to him.'

'He probably knows that already. As Garson said, he removed the recorder because he knows we're on his track.'

'Probably true,' Hargraves admitted; then he sat for a moment and stared in front of him, obviously thinking.

'An idea, sir?' Brice asked hopefully.

'Maybe. Look, one of the puzzling points has been that June Dawson received a call from the murderer whilst we were talking to Kenton. That, we decided, ruled him out. But I've just thought of something. He wasn't with us all the time, you know.'

'Wasn't?' Brice looked surprised. 'I don't recall — But I do!' he exclaimed abruptly, snapping his fingers. 'He left us for a moment or two to turn out the gas burner, or something. But he was only away for a moment or so . . . You can't read anything into that, can you?'

'I can read this much: In that time he could have switched on preset remote-control radio, and then come back to talk to us. The preset radio operated the telephone kiosk recorder. How it switched itself off I don't know, but in these days of electronics that shouldn't present any problem. Automatic stopping switch, perhaps. There we have a possible answer to the problem of June hearing the voice whilst we were actually talking to Kenton . . . Mmm, very interesting.' He stared into space, musing.

'Better get back to the Yard, sir, hadn't we?' Brice said, returning down to earth. 'Something else of interest may have turned up in the meantime.'

Hargraves nodded, whereupon Brice switched on the ignition and they returned swiftly to Whitehall. Hargraves did not expect to find anything interesting upon his return, but in this he was surprised. There was a note waiting for him on his desk. Without taking off his hat and coat he picked it up and read it.

9.30 A.M.

For the Attention of C.I. Hargraves

Urgent 'phone call at the above time, requesting you to visit Mr. Sawley Garson at the earliest moment. Important matter on which you have to be informed.

Central Information.

'Let's go,' Hargraves said briefly, handing the note to Brice. 'Wonder what the scientific bloodhound has got hold of this time?'

Within a very short time they were at

213

Garson's home, and Crowther admitted them. He led the way to the annexed laboratory and there left them. Garson himself, in a stained white overall, came over immediately to greet them.

'I think I've got something, Hargraves,' he said. 'How much it will help you, I don't know — but at least it proves that the man who sent the telephone warnings never really existed.'

'Eh?' Hargraves gave start. 'Dammit, man, I thought you said you had found something to help me! Aren't things difficult enough already without discovering the 'phone caller never existed?'

Garson grinned. 'Anyway, take a look at this . . . ' He led the way to a film projector and slipped in the 'still' mechanism.

'I've spent all night on this job because I thought the sooner we get results the better for everybody. First — take a look at this.'

He drew the blinds over the windows and then switched on the projector. On the screen on the opposite wall, occupying exactly half of it horizontally, appeared a picture resembling a graph — a series of peaks and valleys, with the highest peak of all in the approximate center.

'What's that?' Hargraves demanded, staring. 'Looks like some kind of drawing of a mountain range!'

'That, my earthbound friend, represents visually the peaks and valleys created by a natural speaking voice. It's a sound track, and it is the kind of track used by experts as a specimen. In other words, it is a visual track of a natural human voice.'

'And where does that get us? I'm not very well up in this scientific mumbo-jumbo.'

'Then I'll make it elementary. Take a look at this.'

Along the bottom half of the screen there slid another graph, but this time the peaks and valleys were very different. Some were high beyond the average, whilst the valleys dipped to great depth.

'Now — notice something,' Garson continued, going over to the screen. 'In the top graph — the natural human voice

215

— you will observe that under this enormous magnification the lines are all slightly rippled — wobbly — which is as they should be. The very action of the heart pumping the bloodstream causes that pulsation in the human voice. And there it is, faithfully registered.'

'Uh-huh,' Hargraves agreed, studying the picture. 'Clear enough. What does it all add up to?'

'This! Notice this lower graph? Not a single line wavers. They are all dead straight — and the peaks and valleys are utterly different to those produced by a human voice. Audibly, this lower voice would *sound* all right — quite a normal, soft voice. But *visually*, the trick is betrayed. And where did this lower voice come from? It's part of the voice on the telephone, recorded by the post office engineers on tape, and transposed by me into visual lines. Nothing in that: just a trick of electronics. But the result is obvious.'

Hargraves considered, not at all liking the job of wrestling with a scientific problem. Yet he realized the necessity of it.

'Do you mean,' he said at last, 'that this lower graph, taken from the tape recorder, didn't belong to a voice in the first place?'

'It belonged to an *artificial* voice — one of the neatest tricks I've seen for a long time. In other words, our murderer first drew the voice — which must have taken the hell of a time — on a piece of film. He'd listen to it on a sound projector, no doubt, and correct it until he got it perfect. When it *was* perfect he transferred it to tape. The result was — and is — a soft, modulated voice that never really possessed an owner! Created entirely by scale-drawn lines, which mimic the lines produced by a natural voice. It's done professionally quite a lot, particularly in cartoons. The one flaw is the lack of tremor, which the natural voice always possesses, though it's unnoticed by the ear.'

'Well, I'll be damned,' Hargraves murmured; then he blinked a little as the daylight was restored. 'Thanks a million, Garson. It solves the problem of a mysterious 'other party' having been called in to recite the murderer's message.'

'As I told you,' Garson shrugged, 'no murderer would be crazy enough to entrust anybody with his secret.'

'But the trouble the murderer's taken!' Brice exclaimed. 'It's incredible!'

'It's elaborate — definitely elaborate — but by no means incredible,' Garson said. 'Obviously, we are dealing with a very clever man — whose cleverness may indeed be a ramification of a somewhat unbalanced mind. He plainly knows a good deal about electronics and hypnotism and he's used them to the full. He gambled on the chance that the very complexity of the mystery would make detection of the culprit impossible, especially in regard to the voice. A criminal's ego, once again. But that's where he went wrong. What one scientist can do, Sawley Garson can undo!'

'Things sort of begin to fit in,' Hargraves said, musing. 'I may as well tell you, Garson, that — in my own mind at least — I've as good as settled on Jerome Kenton as the culprit, even though there are several points I can't yet reconcile.'

'Kenton, eh?' Garson lighted a cigarette. 'Why the particular concentration on him? What about Dr. Mason, the hypnotherapist? Isn't there a case for him, too?'

'When weighed against Kenton there isn't. Our latest discovery on Kenton relates to his wife. She died because Sir Robert Dawson, in operating upon her, failed to save her from death. No reflection on Dawson, but imagine the effect on Kenton's mind. He *could* think he had reason to be revenged. First the actual shock of his wife's death, and then this obsession, this fixation, which has grown over the intervening years.'

'And he now thinks his revenge should encompass the entire Dawson family?'

'That's my guess. Elaborate, scientific planning, allied to hypnotism, and carried through with relentless purpose . . . I am assuming incidentally that an unbalanced mind *could* work out the details. What do you say?'

'Definitely. This man is only unbalanced in one direction: he has more than his share of sanity in every other way.'

'My own idea exactly. But now to the snags. We're pretty convinced that the bogus reporter from the *Argus* was the real hypnotist, but how the hell can a blond haired man with dark blue or dark brown eyes match up with Jerome Kenton? In size yes, even in voice, since he has a pleasant baritone, as had the reporter — but his eyes are pale blue or gray. They look nearly transparent. Even if he wore a blond wig, which is quite feasible, he couldn't change the color of his eyes.'

Garson grinned. 'He could, you know. And if you can't think how you must be slipping.'

Hargraves stared, and so for that matter did Brice. Then they looked at each other in bafflement,

'The answer is contact lenses,' the scientist said. 'Just enough room for the pupil to see through, and up and down and horizontal movement of the eye permitted by means of a thin plus sign on the lens. Pigment the rest of the lens to look like the iris of an eye and there you have it. The man wore densely thick glasses, didn't he? That would make the cross on the lens invisible and would also hide a multitude of other imperfections — all the more so because Miss Dawson, the observer with whom we are concerned, wouldn't be looking for such trickery anyway.'

'In fact the whole trick's wonderfully neat,' Hargraves growled. 'I've dealt with plenty of killers in my time, but never one as ingenious — or so thorough as this one . . . In which case it could be Jerome Kenton very easily. It was just the eyes which got me stopped.'

'And one other thing,' Brice remarked, looking at the scientist. 'Do you think the remote control apparatus which controls the recorder could be switched on in an instant and left to its own devices?'

'I see no reason why not,' Garson shrugged. 'Once it is set to its correct wavelength and so forth there's nothing more to do — any more than there is in the case of an ordinary radio set. The recorder is — or *was* — a static object. It would be a different matter if it were mobile, like controlling the movements of a model remote-controlled model air-plane, for instance. Why?'

'When we went to see Kenton,' Hargraves explained, taking up the thread, 'he left us for a moment with an excuse about a gas ring and some cooking, or something. Come to think of it, neither of us *smelled* any cooking but we didn't think anything of it at the time. Kenton came back almost immediately and we thought no more about it. June Dawson received her phone call whilst we were with Kenton, so can it be safely assumed that in that precious moment he switched on the remote control appara-tus, relying on some kind of 'stop' gadget to cut it off when the message had finished?'

'I think,' Garson said, after due consideration, 'that you are safe in your assumption ... ' Then, after a pause, 'And what do you propose to do now? Arrest him?'

Hargraves made a grim face. 'Where's my proof? Although we've learned quite a few things, we haven't yet got the one thing that will permit us to sail in and nab him — and quite frankly, I'll be hanged if I know where we can get that one thing, either. Unless you've any suggestions, Garson?'

'None at all at the moment. On the other hand, Kenton's a very dangerous man to have walking around. Can't you nab him on one of the usual pretexts like income tax default, or something?'

'Unfortunately no. I've examined all possibilities in that direction but Jerome Kenton's quite safe.'

'Mmm, I see your difficulty. And you can't even point to the 'phone box as an accusation because he's moved the one piece of incriminating evidence. And certainly his rooms will be free of anything of a guilty nature . . . Seems to me that the only thing to do is wait for him making the one mistake that all criminals make — overreaching himself.'

'It may be some time before he does that,' Hargraves commented gloomily.

'Perhaps not as long as you think. Remember, he's failed to get June Dawson. Do you think he'll rest content when he realizes that fact?'

'Probably not — but he also knows, as is evidenced by his removing the recorder from the 'phone box — that we're on to him. For that very reason he may not attempt anything further.'

Garson shook his head slowly. 'He knew you were on to him when you called to question him, but that didn't prevent him switching on the remote control radio to the recorder even whilst you were with him. In other words, despite the danger that had suddenly materialized he went on with his plans. You still haven't properly got the measure of a criminal of his sort, Hargraves; the psychological aspect is important. Obsessed as he is, I think he'll try again.'

'Let's hope so,' Hargraves muttered. 'Otherwise we'll have to think of a fresh line of action — and that won't be easy. In the meantime you suggest we just sit down and wait for it?'

'I do — irksome though it may be. If, after a while, he doesn't come out into the open, we'll have to dream up something to make him betray his hand. It won't be easy because he's a damned clever man and a ruthless killer. With existing murders already incriminating him he won't care how many more he commits . . . Anyway, we'll have to see what happens. In the meantime, though I don't want to sound as though I'm teaching you your job, I have some other suggestions.'

'Such as?'

'You already know a thing or two about Kenton's past life — but I wouldn't let it rest there. There must be a good deal more. Find out all you can. Try and discover where he learned so much about radio, sound recording, and so forth. It shouldn't be difficult with routine police methods. Then you'll have everything to pile on top of him when at last you nail him.'

Hargraves nodded. 'I'll do that, Garson — and thanks for the tip. And if you find anything more on the scientific side, be sure to let us know. Okay, sergeant, let's get back to the office and plan our campaign.'

★　★　★

For June Dawson, the knowledge of what had happened to her, and the thought of how her will had been completely overruled by an unknown potential killer, produced a sobering reaction. With the coming of the next day, and with the new shift of men keeping a watch on the house, she had time to think and appreciate how near she had come to death.

She and her mother did not discuss the matter at undue length. In her own mind, June was perfectly sure that some fresh attempt would be made on her life, and for her mother there was the added anxiety of thinking that she too would be a target as well as her daughter. It was small wonder that neither of them said much for fear of disturbing the other; They could only pursue a boring, routine existence, chained to the indoors and forbidden any callers — until gradually, as days went by, their spirits began to rebel against the enforced incarceration.

'I wonder what these fools at Scotland Yard think they are doing?' Lady Dawson exclaimed, on the third day. 'Three days since that attempt on your life, June, and not a thing happens. What's the use of police if they don't do anything?'

'I think they *are* doing something,' June replied seriously. 'We've not the slightest idea how they work, remember, and because we don't see anything it looks as though they've forgotten all about us. I'm sure they haven't. The different relays of men who keep coming to guard the house is proof of that in itself.'

'Well, anyway, it's ridiculous! There ought to be some sort of action!'

For that matter, Chief-Inspector Hargraves was thinking exactly the same thing, but he certainly had not been idle in the interval, whatever Lady Dawson might have thought. Using normal police methods he and Brice between them had unearthed quite a number of facts about Jerome Kenton. In the first place, long before he had taken up the role of knife thrower on the halls, he had been a sound engineer — a maintenance expert in fact for a chain of movie houses, which seemed to explain conclusively where he had derived his knowledge of electronics, sound, and similar subjects. It explained away his know-how on transistor tape recorders, the drawing of sound tracks, and so forth.

It was after his spell as a sound engineer that he became a hypnotist. Here, the evidence was less clear, but at least the indefatigable Brice unearthed the fact that he had once appeared on the halls as the 'Great Mesmo,' until his activities had been banned by the police in case of possible dangerous influence. Thus checked, Kenton then took up the role of knife-thrower.

The connection between the Great Mesmo and Jerome Kenton was not exact, but after a study of dates, times, and the date of police intervention, a logical inference could be drawn. Mesmo and Kenton were the same person.

'Which seems to provide the correct background,' Hargraves said, after a study of the facts.

'Yes, sir,' Brice conceded. 'Just the same — and I don't like saying it — we still haven't any conclusive evidence with which to arrest him.'

'No — so the only thing we can do is gamble. A dangerous gamble, too. Nothing less than the life of June Dawson!'

Brice gave a whistle.

'In other words,' Hargraves continued, 'we shall apparently drop the case entirely. Call off the watchdogs and apparently not do a thing. Gradually, I trust, Kenton will gather courage and come out of his lair. He'll make some kind of move — and from a distance we'll still be watching him. Then, at the right moment, we'll step in.'

'You're going to use June Dawson as bait, then?'

'It's all I can do.' Hargraves got to his feet and began to move around restlessly. 'Don't think I like doing it, but I've no other course. I'm basing everything on the fact that the killer will try yet again to get June, and probably her mother too. Whichever one he attacks we'll be good and ready for him.'

'Yes, sir,' Brice conceded quietly, though inwardly he did vaguely wonder what was going to happen if something misfired and there was yet another killing to add to the list.

'That's it, then,' Hargraves said, with an air of finality. 'I'll call off the men from the Dawson residence, and put them to work watching Kenton's every move.'

'And are you going to tell Mr. Garson of your intentions?'

Hargraves reflected, then he shrugged. 'I wasn't going to, but perhaps I'd better. Seeing as he's helped us so much it's only fair to tell him what's going on.'

Brice nodded in silent relief. Though he had infinite faith in his superior, he also knew his limitations. He felt a good deal safer with the thought of Garson in the picture. There was one man who had a gift for anticipating.

So there and then Hargraves 'phoned the scientist and explained his decision. The scientist listened in silent interest until at length the Chief-Inspector had finished. Then:

'All right, Hargraves, up to you,' he said. 'It certainly seems as though a prod is necessary so far as Kenton is concerned. But watch that girl very carefully. There'll be plenty of trouble yet before you get the evidence you want to make an arrest.'

'I'm prepared for that. From here on it's routine, police work.'

'You hope!' came the rather ambiguous response, and with that Garson rang off.

Hargraves put the telephone down slowly, meditating to himself. That last remark from the scientist had come as something like a cold douche.

★ ★ ★

Naturally, June Dawson was not told directly that she was bait for the killer, but she had commonsense enough to know that she *was* — and indeed her mother openly said so. None of which made any difference to Hargraves' plans. He had the men withdrawn from the Dawson residence and, on the face of it, dropped all interest in the case.

Just the same, men were watching the Dawson home from distance, some of them under the guise of road-menders, painters, and recreation ground gardeners — the recreation ground being only a hundred yards away from the Dawson home . . . still other men kept the vital telephone box under observation, though not ostentatiously — and Jerome Kenton's rooms were likewise watched night and day. With all these men moving on the chessboard Hargraves felt that he had done all he reasonably could to safeguard the girl and leave the way clear for the killer to walk into the trap.

For a day or two nothing happened, and with the slowly increasing sense of security June's desire for change began to become something of an obsession. Still only young, her main desire was to get outside, breathe the fresh air, see the town and the bright lights once again and forget the shadow of a murderer brooding over herself and her mother. Anything in fact, to break the crushing monotony that was stifling her. Although there was no longer a ban on her movements, she could not somehow summon up the necessary courage to leave the comparative security of home.

She was in the midst of trying to make up her mind, three days after the withdrawal of the watchdogs, when to her surprise she had a visitor. None other than Herbert Mason. He came in, quietly smiling, as Baines announced him.

'Why, Herby!' June got to her feet. 'This *is* a surprise!'

'I thought it would be,' he responded, and turning he smiled a greeting to Lady Dawson. 'As a matter of fact I thought it was about time I saw how things were with you. There's a rather slack time at the hospital at the moment, so here I am. Playing truant!'

'I'll tell the headmaster,' June admonished; then she gave a little smile. 'Actually, Herby, it's a tremendous relief seeing you . . . Do sit down, won't you? Surely you're not going to tear off as soon as you've got here?'

'As a matter of fact,' Mason said, glancing at his watch, 'I was wondering if you'd care to come to lunch with me. Or would that be out of order?'

'Why on earth should it be?'

'Well, with various things hanging over you like murder, adjourned inquests, and so forth, I rather wondered. I don't want to be blunt or callous, but the outside world goes on just the same . . . You look as though a change would do you both good.'

'Don't include me in it,' Lady Dawson said, glancing up. 'I admit that it becomes boring in the house, but somehow — just at present — I do not feel I could face the outside world . . . You go, June. As Herby says, the change will do you good. I'll be all right here.'

'Right, then that's settled!' June headed for the door. 'I shan't be long, Herby.'

Nor was she. Within half an hour Herbert Mason's fast car whirled them into the heart of the city towards lunchtime. Another car followed them, even though they were not aware of it. To have a car following in the midst of London traffic is neither here nor there. The car was only a small one, but quite powerful, and contained one occupant. It kept up with Mason's sleek convertible, following it down the main road into town, and thereafter pursuing it until finally Mason drew up outside a smart and exclusive restaurant. The following car swept by, quite unnoticed, but its solitary driver knew exactly what was transpiring.

The one thing that Mason, June, and the pursuing driver did not notice was a black saloon, also in pursuit. It went past the restaurant as Mason and the girl alighted, and then carried on up a side street. There it stopped and two plain clothes men looked inquiringly at one another.

'Okay, keep on the job,' one of them said at length, opening the door. 'I'll see you later.'

In the meantime, holding June's arm protectively, Mason was leading the way into the warm cosiness of the restaurant and selected a quiet corner table. He drew forth a chair for her. He did not say anything until the luncheon order had been given, then he looked at the girl seriously, a wealth of earnestness in his dark blue eyes.

'In the mood for talking?' he inquired gently. 'Or would you rather just —think?'

'Thinking won't do me any good, Herby. I'd rather not. It might prove too depressing. Why do you ask? Is there something particular you wish to say to me?'

'There is — and I'm not quite sure how to say it.' Mason avoided looking at the girl directly. I've had it over with myself a lot these last few days, and I don't quite know what to do about it. It'll sound selfish, concentrating on my own interests at a time when you're deeply worried. I mean, Gerald, Trudy, and your dad, all murdered — '

'You might as well include me, too,' June added absently. 'I was nearly finished off the other night.'

Mason started. 'You too? How do you mean? There hasn't been an attack made on *your* life as well, surely?'

'There has, you know. Naturally, you won't know anything about it because I haven't seen you in the interval, and the business was kept out of the papers. It was all quite horrifyingly real, none the less.'

'What happened?' Mason demanded.

June gave the details and Mason sat listening attentively. Now and again his eyes strayed to the incoming diners who took up tables round and about, but otherwise his attention to the girl was complete.

'So *that's* what happened!' he said finally, as the girl finished talking. 'Thank God that fellow Garson foresaw the trick with the television, or the game would have been up for you.' Mason ate in silence for a moment or two, thinking. 'You know, June, I'm inclined to agree with your mother. It's about time the police got some action on this business instead of leaving you on the edge of a volcano in this fashion.'

'Nothing I can do about it. They work in a mysterious way their wonders to perform.' June shrugged. 'Anyway, let's try and forget it for the moment. Let me thank you for lifting me out of an ocean of gloom and bringing me to lunch as you have . . . What was it you wanted to talk to me about when we got off the subject?'

'Well, I was thinking that . . . ' Mason hesitated, clearly at a loss for words: then suddenly he came straight to the point. 'Look, June, you know I was going to marry poor Trudy. After — after what happened I'm left without anybody. I wondered if you and I — I'm more than fond of you, and always have been, but I don't want you to think there's any question of 'second best' or anything like that. I want you for yourself alone. I was fond of you even when I was engaged to Trudy — but I obviously couldn't marry two girls, and Trudy happened to come first into my life. It's different now. She's — she's gone. And you're still here.'

June did not say anything. She went on eating, her eyes on her plate.

'The way things are you could certainly do with a man in your life,' Mason continued, with a touch of desperation. 'A man who could perhaps do more than the police seem to be doing in tracking down this killer . . . '

'You think you could do something?' June asked. 'What, for instance?'

'Well, I don't know exactly, but anyway it would lighten the load if you cared to share it with me . . . That is unless there is a man in your life already?'

June laughed gently and gripped

Mason's hand across the table.

'No, there isn't anybody else, Herby — nobody that matters, anyhow. Thanks for wanting to take care of me,' she added seriously. 'You'll never know how much I appreciate that. And I think it's just what Trudy would agree to. I know the kind of man you are, and that's an enormous advantage to any girl.'

'Fine!' Mason relaxed and gently mopped his brow. 'Warm in this restaurant, isn't it?'

'I hadn't noticed,' June smiled.

Mason smiled broadly; then from that moment onwards, until the lunch was finished, the conversation covered a variety of subjects. So absorbed were they both that the restaurant might have been empty for all the notice they took of the diners on all sides of them. Certainly neither of them even glanced towards a man nearby, busy with a chop — and even if they had glanced neither would have recognized him in his horn-rimmed glasses. But it did seem that his glasses were directed towards them through long periods as though he were studying them intently.

It was June's confession that she had a developing headache that finally led her and Herbert Mason outside to the fresh air. Beside his car they stopped and June fingered her forehead gently.

'Sure you're all right?' Mason asked in concern.

'Yes, sure . . . ' June managed a smile. 'It's going off now. Must have been the heat of that restaurant: it was warmer than I imagined. I'll be all right.'

Mason nodded seriously. 'There was quite a lot more I wanted to say to you, June — but anyway we'll be seeing a good deal of each other from now on. Unfortunately, the demands on my time at the hospital don't give me much chance to see you, but we'll do our best. Now look — about this headache of yours. Shall I take you straight home?'

'Good heavens no, thanks all the same. I'll take a walk in the fresh air and have a look at some of the shops. I feel just like a prisoner out on parole.'

'You're *sure* you'll be all right?'

'Certainly I will. My headache's nearly

gone now, and I'm surrounded by people as far as personal safety is concerned.'

'I wish I didn't have to go,' Mason muttered, 'but I've got to get along. As I told you, I took time out — and I daren't take any more.'

'I quite understand, Herby. You go. When you have a moment to spare give me a ring and we'll fix up something.'

'Fair enough. I'll do that.'

Mason climbed into his convertible, settled at the wheel, then with a wave he drew away from the kerb. June watched him go, until presently his car was lost in the flow of city traffic. Slowly she turned and began to walk, pondering to herself as she went. And, strangely enough, her thoughts were not on Herbert Mason and his avowal of love for her, but upon an address in Notting Hill Gate. An address which in the normal way she did not even know — the address of a place she had never seen, yet which for some obscure reason demanded all her interest and concentration.

She glanced at her watch: it was 1.15.

For another half hour she continued to wander along the busy street, glancing in the shop windows and trying to sort out her curious mental perturbations at the same time. Certainly she did not really see anything in the shop windows — she kept thinking of 29 Harrison Avenue, Notting Hill Gate — an address she had never known before this moment. She knew in spite of everything that she had to visit it.

At precisely 1.45 she made up her mind. She stepped to the kerb, signaled a taxi, and gave her instructions to the driver.

'29 Harrison Avenue, Notting Hill Gate, as fast as you can.'

'Okay, lady.'

He slammed the rear door upon her and then settled in the leather upholstery. Thereafter, as the journey was made, she sat gazing rather vacantly in front of her, her view limited to the driver's broad, leather-coated back. When at length the fairly long trip was complete the driver looked about him in Harrison Avenue, particularly at No. 29 — then he stopped and came round to open the door.

'We're there, lady,' he announced, a rather puzzled look on his beefy face. 'I suppose you've got the right address? From the look of things there ain't anybody living in No. 29. An empty bungalow . . .'

June, still with a faraway look in her eyes, merely shrugged and climbed out of the taxi to the sidewalk.

'It doesn't matter,' she said. 'I particularly wanted this address. How much do I owe you?'

The driver glanced at the meter, told her the amount registered, and then waited whilst she delved into her handbag.

'Thanks lady.' He took the money she gave him. 'I know it's no business of mine, but how are you going to get back into town? Do you want me to wait for you?'

'No, you needn't wait, thank you.'

With that she turned and walked slowly away, studying the bungalow of No. 29 as she did so. The taxi driver waited a moment or two, watching her, then with a shrug and muttering something about women he climbed back into the driver's seat and headed back for town. Meanwhile, June had come to a stop outside No. 29, studying the weed-smothered garden, the grimy windows, and general air of neglect. The bungalow was quite a big one, detached from its trim neighbors, and with a little effort applied to it could probably be made into something really worthwhile.

Not that these points interested June. She was obsessed with one thought only: she must enter the bungalow by the back door and go through into the front room. She knew she had that to do. Nothing else in the world really seemed to count at the moment except that.

Unlatching the gate she went up the front path, and then detoured round the side of the bungalow to the rear. It should have surprised her to discover, when she tried the main back door, that it was not bolted. A gentle push, and it swung open on its hinges.

On the step she stopped, staring into the dusty emptiness of what would normally be the kitchen. There was not a sound. Only the dank, depressing gloom of the winter afternoon . . . Under an impulse that was not her own she went slowly into the kitchen and, without looking about her, went through it to the bare-boarded hall. From this led the main front room, which she felt so compelled to visit.

Her pace slowed slightly as she approached it, as though she had an instinctive conviction that all was not well. Then suddenly, before she could cross the threshold of the front room, a figure whirled from the gloom near the base of the stairs, grabbed her round the waist, and whirled her backwards helplessly.

★　　★　　★

It was in the early afternoon when one of the p.c. men detailed to keep observation on June Dawson came rapidly into Hargraves' office. The Chief-Inspector looked up sharply, sensing that all was not as it should be.

'Well, Bradshaw? Something happened?'

'It may have done, sir; I can't be quite sure. But I thought I had better report it right away. Miss Dawson left the house and went to lunch with a tall, dark-headed fellow who seemed pretty intimate with her.'

'Sounds like Dr. Mason,' Brice put in, listening.

'And what happened?' Hargraves questioned.

'We tailed them to a restaurant, and saw them come out again. Then Miss Dawson parted from the tall fellow and went looking at the stores in the main street. Round about quarter to two she suddenly seemed to decide on something for she called a taxi and — '

'Which you followed, I hope!' Hargraves was looking grim.

'Well, sir, we tried to — but unfortunately we lost them at the traffic lights. We were held up, and they went on — northwards. We just couldn't find them again, so I came back to report. Miss Dawson may be taking an innocent journey, of course — '

'And maybe not!' Hargraves snapped.

'Damn the luck: Did you get the taxi's number?'

'I did, sir.' Bradshaw was feeling immensely relieved that Hargraves was not wiping the floor with him. He glanced at his notebook. 'Er — Hackney Carriage, 0 stroke 712. Usual London taxi.'

'Okay. I'll trace the driver and find where Miss Dawson went. Anything else?'

'Yes, sir. When Miss Dawson and the tall fellow left the Dawson house in his car another car started to follow them. It came from a nearby avenue somewhere and kept on their tail all the way to the restaurant, after which it went straight on and nothing more seemed to happen. It was probably coincidence: somebody going in the same direction, I mean. We took the number, just in case . . . AY 427. A rather ancient car, but pretty fast none the less.'

'Did you notice who was in it?'

'Apparently just one man, sir — the driver. He had a soft hat on. We were so busy watching Miss Dawson and her friend we didn't bother about the other car when it went straight on past the restaurant.'

'Mmm ... ' Hargraves growled. 'All right, Bradshaw — thanks. Get back to the Dawson residence and continue to keep it under surveillance until you get further instructions.'

'Right, sir.'

Bradshaw went out and Hargraves, in an obviously grim mood, picked up the telephone and contacted main switchboard.

'Get me the London Taxicab Company — quickly as you can.' He put the telephone down again and stroked his underlip uncertainly.

'I shouldn't worry too much about it, sir,' Brice commented. 'I should think June Dawson had a perfectly normal reason for what she did.'

'I hope to heaven you're right — but just at present she's in such danger that we can't afford to have our eyes off her for a moment. If anything's gone wrong and I've exposed her to danger through taking a gamble, I'll never forgive myself! So she went to dinner with Herbert

248

Mason, did she?'

'We don't know it was him.'

'No, but it's a reasonable assumption. You don't go to lunch with somebody who calls at your house unless they're a pretty close friend. It'd be Mason all right . . . In fact I'll check on it right now, and be sure.'

Again he picked up the 'phone, looked down his sheet of relevant phone numbers, and then dialed St. Luke's Hospital. Response was immediate, but to bring Herbert Mason to the 'phone took some time.

'Yes, inspector?' came his voice at last. 'This is a bit of a surprise, I can tell you.'

'Sorry to interrupt your work, doctor,' Hargraves said, 'but I'd like you to settle something for me . . . Did you take Miss Dawson to lunch today?'

'As a matter of fact I did. Do you mind?'

'On the contrary: you are a free agent. Might I ask where you left Miss Dawson?'

'Why?' Mason's voice suddenly changed. 'Has something happened to her?'

'Not as far as I know. I repeat: where

did you leave her?'

'Outside the restaurant, after we'd had lunch. Rocarti's in The Winery. On the main Hammersmith Road . . . What *is* all this, inspector? How does it happen that you know our movements?'

'We're still on the case, Dr. Mason, so naturally we have tabs on all the main protagonists.'

'Well, I'm afraid that's all I can tell you. I'd have stayed with June but I had to get back to the hospital. She complained of a headache, so naturally I didn't feel too comfortable about her.'

'Which is quite understandable, doctor. Well, thanks for your information. I just wanted to know.'

'I still can't think why. I think you know more than you're telling me. *Has* anything happened to June?'

'Not that I know of,' Hargraves answered quietly. 'I've said that already, and I'm sticking to it. Good bye for now, doctor.'

He rang off to avoid any more questions; then picked up the second telephone as it buzzed noisily.

'Yes? Hargraves here.'

'Your call to the London Taxi Company, inspector. You're through to them now.'

'Okay, put them on — and while I'm talking to them get me the Central Car Licence Offices.'

'Right, sir.'

The 'phone clicked and the London Taxicab Company was on the line — which as far as Hargraves was concerned, was only the beginning. In all, it took a good ten minutes before the rank containing cab No. 0/712 had been located, and its driver contacted. As it happened, his taxi was back on the stand, and he came immediately to the 'phone.

Hargraves identified himself, then: 'A little while ago, round about quarter to two, you picked up a young woman, fairly tall, blonde, with hazel eyes. In the main Hammersmith High Street. You remember?'

'Yes, sir, I remember.' The driver had already been informed that it was Scotland Yard who wanted the information, and his voice was duly respectful. 'I remember it quite well. She was the last fare I took.'

'Good. What was her destination?'

'29 Harrison Avenue, Notting Hill Gate. It was an empty bungalow. I asked her if I should wait and bring her back into town, but she said it didn't matter. That's all I know, inspector.'

'You've done very well, driver. Thank you . . . Oh, tell me. How did this young woman seem? Was she distraught in any way? Did she seem anxious, composed, or what?'

'As a matter of fact she looked rather dazed to me, and she had a way of looking in front of her as though she wasn't quite sure what she was doing. Just as though she'd had a shock — or was ill or something. That's why I suggested I wait and take her back into town. I felt a bit concerned, but since she seemed to know quite well what she was doing it was really none of my business.'

'I quite understand . . . Thanks very much. Good bye.'

Hargraves rang off and then sat pondering. Presently he raised his eyes to meet the inquiring ones of Brice.

'Just why,' Hargraves mused, 'should June Dawson suddenly take it into her head to go to 29 Harrison Avenue, Notting Hill Gate?'

'Where?' Brice looked puzzled.

'We haven't got such an address anywhere connected with this case, have we, Harry?'

'No, sir. I never even heard of it.'

'Queer! June seemed quite determined to go there — took a taxi to do it, and yet when she gets there the damned place is empty. According to the driver she had a curiously dazed expression, and according to Dr. Mason she had a headache . . . ' Hargraves got to his feet in sudden urgency. 'We'd better get out to that address immediately, Harry. A combination of a headache and a dazed look might spell hypnotism — '

The telephone rang and Hargraves snatched it up with one hand while he took down his overcoat from the stand with the other.

'Hargraves here.'

'That call to the licensing authorities,

sir. You're through.'

Hargraves sighed. 'Okay . . . Hello? I want the owner of the following licence quickly, please. AY 427.'

'If you hang on, we'll trace it in a moment.'

'Right.'

Hargraves had struggled into his hat and coat by he time the answer came through.

'The holder of that licence is Jerome Trenton, 22 Porlock Avenue, West Central.'

'Thanks,' Hargraves said briefly, and put the phone down. Then Brice, who had overheard the conversation, made an observation.

'So, Kenton chases June and Dr. Mason through the city, and the police chase both of them. And our boys concentrated on June, whereas it might have been a better bet to concentrate on Kenton.'

'Uh-huh. What I'm wondering is: why didn't the boys we've got watching *Kenton* report something? Unless he somehow gave them the slip — Anyway, no time now to try and sort that out. We want to get out to Notting Hill Gate and see what happened to the girl friend. Let's go.'

They whirled out of the office, and in a matter of minutes were on their way. Brice did not spare the gas and in less than fifteen minutes they were in the Notting Hill Gate area. Here they lost a bit of time finding Harrison Avenue, but eventually they located and swept into it. With a squeak of brakes Brice drew up outside No. 29.

'Doesn't look to be much going on,' Brice commented. 'What the devil should June Dawson want to come to an empty bungalow for?'

'The only answer is that she was mentally compelled to, Harry. And, incidentally, I'm getting worried — particularly by the fact that she spent lunch with a hypnotherapist.'

'But, sir, you don't mean that after all the evidence we've collected, you're going to shift your viewpoint?' Brice was staring in amazement. 'You haven't suddenly decided that Herbert Mason is the murderer?'

'Sometimes things are forced on one, Harry, and one just has to accept them . . . However, let's see what we can find out.'

Hargraves opened the car door and stepped out. Together, he and Brice approached the bungalow slowly, wary for anything that might happen — and abruptly they paused as they saw the front door opening.

'Look out,' Hargraves said curtly. 'Anything might happen.'

Within a moment or two both Hargraves and Brice realized that their fears were groundless. From the front doorway there emerged the recognizable figure of June Dawson and, holding tightly onto her arm to support her, there came Sawley Garson.

8

'Surprised?' Garson asked dryly, as the two men came up the path towards him.

'What do you think?' Hargraves demanded. 'How the devil did you get here, anyway?'

'I'll tell you in a while. Since you are here, come back inside and let me show you something.'

Hargraves nodded and glanced at the girl. She gave him a faintly puzzled smile. In appearance she looked desperately tired, even on the verge of a faint, had not Garson kept his grip upon her.

'June will be all right in a while,' the scientist said, seeing Hargraves' look of concern as he led her back into the dim hall. 'Hypnotism and shock are responsible for her present condition . . . Now, let me show you something.'

'Just a minute,' Brice said, checking his advance. 'There's a folding chair in the car boot. I'll nip back and get it, then you can sit down and rest, Miss Dawson.'

She nodded her thanks. Hargraves looked at Garson critically.

'I'm still waiting, Garson. What's the explanation of all this?'

'I begin to think I shall never be out of Mr. Garson's debt,' June said. 'This is the second time he's saved me from being killed — '

'Killed!' Hargraves exclaimed. 'In here? In this place? Is that what you mean?'

'Just as well I kept track of things myself whilst the police were chasing rainbows,' Garson commented. Otherwise, Miss Dawson would certainly be dead by now.'

Hargraves frowned, but whatever he intended saying was interrupted as Brice returned. He extended the folding chair and June sank down onto it thankfully.

'Now,' Garson said, moving to the door of the front room. 'Take a look at this . . . '

For some reason he tugged off his overcoat and tossed it through the doorway. The moment he did so there was the sharp report of a gun. Hargraves and Brice both blinked, then watched as, going on his hands and knees and keeping well down near the floor, the scientist retrieved his coat and examined it. Finally he pointed significantly to a bullet hole torn in the fabric.

'Satisfied?' he asked, putting the coat on again. 'I was intending to get you here to examine this lot, but you saved me the job. You can see what would have happened had Miss Dawson stepped over the threshold. The bullet would have shot her right through the heart. It's been carefully planned to do just that. If not the heart, then it would certainly have inflicted a fatal wound. She'd be unable to call for help: nobody around here would bother with an empty bungalow. You can grasp the general setup for yourself.'

'What I don't grasp,' Hargraves said, 'is how the firing was arranged.'

'Oh, that! Simple — selenium cell connected to a revolver trigger. Come and have a look. Keep low down to the floor. I don't think the thing will fire again, but it's as well to be on the safe side.'

On hands and knees the three men

crept into the front room and then stood up. Garson nodded towards the corner facing the door. There, in the dim light, standing on a somewhat rusty photo-graphic tripod — apparently an old light-stand — was a .32 automatic, securely fastened to the tripod head with a home-made metal clamp. On one of the legs of the tripod a small box-like affair was soldered, and from it a length of wire ran, which fastened finally, caliper-fashion, to the trigger of the gun. Yet another length of wire ran from the box to the corner on the same side as the doorway and this connected eventually with a small tube-like object with a lens in front. The lens faced the door at about four and half feet from the floor.

'Get it?' the scientist asked, as Har-graves pondered.

'I think so. That lens thing is a selenium cell emitting a beam across the doorway. When anything blocks the beam the mechanism in that box on the tripod works instantly. In this case the calliper wire fires the trigger of the automatic, which is aimed to shoot anybody in the doorway. Nothing more than a lethal booby-trap.'

'Exactly. Aimed, my friend, to shoot somebody about five feet eight inches tall directly in the heart. Our killer knows Miss Dawson's measurements exactly — her height, anyway.'

'Absolutely devilish!' Hargraves muttered.

'And ingenious,' Garson added. 'But by no means original. The selenium cell notion is not new. Lots of garages these days have their doors opened by the driver passing his car in front of the beam, which automatically opens the doors. I do it myself, in fact. This is merely a different version of the same principle. Selenium cells are used, too, in the projection of sound films, and that again suggests somebody who is used to handling this type of apparatus.'

Hargraves nodded slowly. Garson had said everything but the name of Jerome Kenton.

'And here's a tripod which can also hold a spotlight,' Garson added. 'Remember the three holes we found in the roadway on the south coast road? I'll gamble the measurement will show this was the same tripod . . . As to the rest — Well, once again we have the case of a man who doesn't seem to exist. He kills, but is never near the crime. It's all thought out in advance.'

'Exactly,' Hargraves nodded. 'And Miss Dawson came here because of hypnotic compulsion?'

'That seems to be it. The chance to give the hypnotic order was held in abeyance until Miss Dawson herself made a move. When it finally came she went to a restaurant — and that was where the order was issued. It must have been there for the simple reason that it couldn't have been anywhere else.'

'I'd like to discuss that with you, Garson — but first, tell me how you come to be here.'

'I'll explain that in your office. Right now I think we should take Miss Dawson home and give her a chance to recover from her ordeal.'

Hargraves nodded and helped the girl to her feet.

'Better take this tackle as well,' the scientist added. 'You'll need it for evidence. Load up your car. I'll take Miss Dawson in my own bus: it's parked in the next street.'

Hargraves did not ask any questions: he was pretty confident he would get all the answers later on in any case. He helped Brice to dismantle the murderous apparatus and then it was dumped into the police car. Finally, with June in the scientist's car, the return to the city center was commenced in the dying light of the winter afternoon.

'I think,' Garson said, as June finally entered her home, 'that you will be quite safe at home here, even without guard. You take my assurance on that, Miss Dawson?'

She nodded slowly. 'If you say so. Quite frankly, I've more faith in you than the police — chiefly because you don't have to cling to rigid regulations. But I need hardly add that I'll be glad when this horrible business is cleared up once and for all.'

'You yourself may be instrumental in

bringing that about,' Garson replied. 'Anyhow, more of that later, and for the time being don't go out unless you have to.'

On that, Garson departed, leading the way thereafter with his car to Scotland Yard. Once back in the office — and with the evidence from the empty bungalow unloaded — Hargraves sat back in his chair and raised an inquiring eyebrow.

'Well, Garson, let's have the facts. For you to steal a march on the police isn't new, but at least I'd like to know how you do it.'

'And you shall!' Garson rubbed his ginger hair thoughtfully and then lighted a cigarette. 'Here it is in a nutshell. From the moment you told me you suspected Jerome Kenton, and informed me of the evidence you had gathered against him, I adopted my usual principle and concentrated solely on that one person, seeking a way to trip him up. I never, so to speak, have taken my eyes off him for the last fortnight.'

'In other words, you've been a watch-dog?'

'You might call it that, yes. Every morning when he has left his rooms I watched him. More than that, I was always on his track. I followed him and his car to the theater for rehearsals; I went to the same café for lunch. I came back with him — but I had it so arranged that he was never aware of it. As you know, I've forgotten more about shadowing than your men ever learned.'

'I know,' Hargraves admitted, discomfited. 'So? What then?'

'Kenton didn't do anything interesting until last Saturday afternoon; then he went straight from the theater to that bungalow in Notting Hill Gate. He let himself in, so I presumed he owned the place. I made it my business to find out later on if he really did own it — and my belief was justified. He must have bought it at some time, probably intending to move into it when the time is opportune . . .

'By night, I made it my business to look the place over. That was easy enough when Kenton was otherwise engaged at the theater in the evening. At that time it was totally empty and contained not a single suspicious thing. So I returned to the job of watching his every move.'

'I think I should point out,' Hargraves remarked 'that I have men on the watch too, observing Kenton's movements. They have never reported anything unusual to me.'

'Can't blame them. Kenton has made no really suspicious moves — not the kind that would excite two down-to-earth officers of the law, anyway. I've been extra thorough, remember . . . However, on Monday last, after an afternoon matinée at the theater, he nipped up to the bungalow and, in the fading light, I was able to watch him unload quite a pile of equipment from that car of his. Some of it he took into the bungalow, then brought it out again, evidently as unsatisfactory. To cut a long story short, when I came to examine the place again, I found the layout exactly as you found it tonight. Plainly, trouble was coming.'

'You knew that long ago what was intended, yet never informed me!' Hargraves complained.

'Our object is to catch him red-handed:

you said so yourself long ago, so I decided to wait for that opportunity. Nothing more happened until today . . . Oh, yes, there's one item I forgot. Kenton went early this morning to St. Luke's hospital, before he went to the theater.'

'He what?' Hargraves gave a start and looked at Brice.

Garson repeated the statement, and then added, 'It was not within my province to inquire *why* he went, but in view of what happened later I'd say that he went to see Dr. Mason . . . Anyhow, I followed Kenton when he left the hospital, and he went straight to the Dawson home, taking up position a few avenues away, but at such an angle he could see the residence. He — and I — saw Dr. Mason arrive, and we saw June go out with Mason. Kenton followed them, and they entered a restaurant in the city. I waited long enough to see Kenton, a little while after, also enter the restaurant in dark glasses — '

'Dark glasses!' Hargraves repeated. What the devil would he want those for, in a restaurant?'

'Think, inspector — think. June had already seen him as the bogus reporter from the *Argus* — '

'Yes, but not as *Kenton*. She'd never know him in the ordinary way.'

'She might — and anyway, Kenton wasn't taking the risk, that's clear. But let me get on, will you? I had the idea that Kenton had gained his object and that the next move might be at the bungalow in Notting Hill — so I went there and waited for something to happen. Sure enough, June eventually arrived and I was able to save her. The rest you know.'

'Not quite. There's the hell of a lot I don't know!' Hargraves said bitterly. 'This tie-up between Kenton and the St Luke's Hospital has got me stopped! Don't tell me we've got *two* killers.'

'I don't think so for a moment — but I *do* think we are dealing with a master hypnotist who has a scientific brain and a ruthless determination to kill. Kenton must have realized he'd failed to kill June with the television when no report of it appeared in the newspapers. Reason it from his angle: what must he do?

268

Obviously get the girl into the open somehow. He couldn't do it himself so he did the next best thing — '

'He used Mason!'

'Precisely!'

'But Mason's a hypnotist too! He wouldn't for a moment obey a mental command from somebody else. He'd be too much on the alert for that.'

'Would he?' Garson shook his head slowly. 'You don't realize what immense mental control this Kenton madman has, Hargraves. There have only been one or two like him in all history, mental freaks able to implant thoughts and suggestions directly into the mind — like the notorious Svengali. He's all the more deadly because he makes use of a force which few people understand, or can resist. Look — get Mason over here and let me question him. I'd like to study him in my own way, too. Slowly but surely we're getting to the root of this problem and I fancy the next move will be the final one — and *we'll* make it. All right, get Mason if you can.'

Hargraves reached for the telephone,

presently contacted the hospital, and finally Herbert Mason himself.

'Hargraves here again,' the inspector said affably. 'Can you spare the time for a few words with me, doctor? It's very important.'

'How important? Nothing's happened to June, has it?'

Hargraves frowned. 'June Dawson's welfare seems to have become an obsession with you, doesn't it?'

'You can't blame me for that, surely, especially when she means so much to me.'

'So much to you? The sister of your late fiancée? I can understand a certain amount of affection, but — '

'There's a reason,' Mason's voice interrupted. 'You say you want me to come and see you? Well — er — '

'It's about June, doctor, and nothing's happened to her so don't start getting alarmed.'

'Well — er — All right, I'll spare the time. I'll be there in about fifteen minutes.'

Hargraves smiled and rang off. In the

fifteen minutes Garson busied himself measuring the stride of the tripod feet and comparing the figures with those written down in his notebook.

'Exactly the same!' he exulted. 'Definitely we are getting somewhere, Hargraves. The chances of a tripod's extended legs being duplicated are about a million to one against. Every one of them has a different straddle . . . '

'Better get some tea from the canteen, Harry,' Hargraves said. 'I need it, and an extra one for Mason. It'll help put him at his ease. And I'm to leave the questioning to you, Garson?'

'Entirely. I think I know what to fish for.'

And, true to his promise, Mason presently put in an appearance. He nodded to the inspector and Brice, and then looked in polite interest at Garson.

'Sawley Garson,' Hargraves introduced. 'A scientist who helps us now and again when a case goes into more technical side channels than we expect.'

'Have a seat, doctor,' the scientist invited. 'In fact have a cup of tea. We're not so hard-hearted at Scotland Yard as some people choose to think . . . Now, as the inspector has told you, I'm an outside man.'

'I see . . . I think.' Mason took a seat, his dark blue eyes shifting from one to the other.

'I'm going to ask a few pertinent questions, doctor, and I hope you'll oblige with sensible answers.' Garson spread his hands. 'Right?'

'I'll do my best.' Mason stirred his tea. 'What do you want to know?'

'Just this. What prompted you to call on Miss June Dawson this morning?'

'Is that really any concern of yours, Mr. Garson?'

'Definitely it is! Because Miss Dawson met you, and went out to lunch with you, she nearly lost her life later in the afternoon. If she had *not* gone out it wouldn't have happened . . . '

'So another attempt *has* been made!' Mason exclaimed. 'Inspector, you led me to believe — '

'I said that June Dawson is safe at home, doctor — or words to that effect.

Anyway, she is. This interview is Mr. Garson's idea, not mine. I'd suggest you answer his questions accurately, no matter how odd or personal they may seem. Many of them may be vital.'

Mason shrugged. 'All right — no reason why I should make myself difficult. I went to see June because I thought it was about time I did. I don't suppose it matters much as far as you are concerned, but I asked her to become engaged to me in place of her murdered sister Trudy.'

'I see . . . ' Garson rubbed his ginger thatch. 'And did you wake up with this resolve, or did it come to you during the morning?'

'I — er — That's a damned odd question. As a matter of fact I thought of it during the morning, and then later on I implemented it.'

'I would suggest that you thought of it after you had seen your patients. Am I right?'

Mason thought for a moment. 'Well, yes, come to think of it. Look here, what are you getting at?'

'You'll see in a moment . . . Have you a patient named Jerome Kenton?'

'Not that I can recall,' Mason said, thinking. 'I could check the list, but I don't recall the name.'

'Probably an assumed name was used,' Garson said. 'Never mind it, doctor. Let's try something else — Can you recall the patients you saw this morning?'

'I think so. There weren't very many. My job is that of consulting hypnotherapist. Sometimes there are outside patients who come specially to see me regarding the hypnotherapy treatment of some disease or other, and — '

'Then an outsider could come to the hospital, ask to see you, and secure your advice?'

'It often happens, though I prefer an appointment.' Mason gave a rather rueful smile. 'Unfortunately I haven't yet reached such high eminence that I can demand appointments only.'

'All right: we've established the basic facts. Now, can you remember if a medium sized man called upon you this morning? A man with rather colorless eyes? Aged say around fifty?'

Mason did not even hesitate. 'Yes, there was such a man. He wanted to know if he could have treatment for arthritis by hypnotherapy. He came for the first check-up. His name was . . . Er — Tate. Douglas Tate.'

'Actually it was Jerome Kenton, the murderer of your fiancée, Sir Robert, and Gerald Dawson,' Garson said grimly. 'And you have been the tool of his will without being aware of it. Bit of a shock, isn't it?'

'*I* have? But — but how do you mean? I'm afraid I don't understand.'

'Then I'll make it plainer, doctor. You were hypnotized by this man — if one can call him a man — into deciding to visit June this morning and take her out to lunch. Afterwards, you left her, making work at the hospital your excuse for doing so.'

'Absurd!' Mason said flatly. 'Absolutely absurd! Hypnotized indeed! I am a hypnotist myself, and a busy hospital office is no place for such an art! You must be wrong somewhere, Mr. Garson.'

'I am not wrong. As I have said before, this man Kenton is a master-hypnotist. He has his art developed to a very high degree. You're a hypnotist yourself. Do you not agree that you could — if so motivated — force anybody to do anything by forcing the correct mental compulsion upon them?'

'It would depend on the subject. If there was resistance — '

'Why should there be, when the victim doesn't know that mental compulsion is intended? You were not aware of what Jerome Kenton intended to do to you — yet during the time you interviewed him, during the time you were looking at him, into his eyes, he was forcing upon you certain mental commands, which you carried out to the letter. Since they were pleasant orders you thought them your own idea, but you carried them out just the same.'

'I still can't hardly believe it, even though I suppose it is possible to someone with freakish powers and a mastery of the art. Let us amend it and say it wasn't hypnotism as such: it was mental suggestion, which I unwittingly accepted.'

'All right,' Garson conceded. 'After that, you decided on your moves after the patients — Kenton amongst them — had left you. To me, that seems quite conclusive.'

'And what happened after that?' Mason asked. 'Everything was perfectly normal in the restaurant — though I admit I left June without hardly realizing why I did so. With the danger to her life it would probably have been better if I'd stuck by her. You say that June nearly lost her life because she went out with me. What took place exactly? I didn't notice anything unusual in the restaurant.'

'You were not intended to; but you can take it for granted that Kenton entered that restaurant and sat somewhere near, where he could see Miss June. He hypnotically commanded her to go to an address in Notting Hill Gate at 1.45 this afternoon. And she went. I know, because I kept track of her. And thank heaven I did!'

'What kind of a devil *is* this man? His

hypnotism must be of the most dangerous order, unknown to conventional science!'

'No doubt of that,' Garson agreed. 'It seems probable that he used hypnosis this time even whilst wearing dark glasses. That is not impossible, particularly with the kind of oppressive will he seems to have.'

'But his reason?' Mason demanded. 'Why does he do this sort of thing? Is he crazy, or what?'

'Not crazy in the accepted sense, but he's certainly tremendously vindictive.'

'Why on earth don't you — or rather the police — have him arrested? Apart from the crimes he's committed already, think how he must be influencing the general public. He's a positive scourge.'

'Don't worry, doctor, we'll get him — *and* we'll put him where he won't be able to do any more damage.'

'Thank heaven for that!' Mason pinched finger and thumb to his eyes. Then suddenly he seemed to think of something for he looked up sharply. 'Come to think of it, this man Kenton — or whatever he's called — was at Warlock's party! I've only just remembered. I *thought* I'd seen him before when he came to the hospital for treatment.'

'It was at that party, so we think,' Hargraves put in, 'that he had the opportunity to poison Trudy. And that raises another question. Trudy died from an overdose of hyoscyamus. Is hyoscyamus easy or difficult to obtain, doctor?'

'Not too difficult, being an opiate — but the poison register would have to be signed. Why?'

'Tell me . . . ' Hargraves frowned as he thought something out. 'Tell me, is today the only time Kenton has been to see you?'

'Well, no. He's come at infrequent intervals, under the order of his own doctor who's treating him for arthritis . . . ' Mason gave a grim look. 'You're not suggesting that he's used his hypnotic powers on me on *other* occasions too, are you?'

'I'm suggesting that, knowing the deadly power he possesses, he has used it on many occasions to gain his own ends. So long as the law of self-preservation is not jeopardized he can get away with almost anything. What would there be to prevent him, on some occasion, commanding you to give him some hyoscyamus? What would there be to prevent you doing just that? With the entire resources of the hospital around you, and no questions asked, you could easily do it.'

'Yes ... Yes, I suppose I could.' Mason's face was haggard. 'I can't think why such a master of hypnotism decided on poison in the case of Trudy. It seems ... incongruous, somehow.'

'Maybe it suited his purpose better, or something.'

'It's a terrible thing, inspector, to think that I might have been responsible, however remotely, for Trudy's death — by perhaps handing on the poison, all unknowingly.'

Hargraves shrugged. 'I don't say it *is* so, doctor, but we can certainly count it as a possibility. Trudy's was the one case where Kenton adopted what we might call 'straightforward' murder. Don't let it worry you too much: you were an entirely unwitting party. We'll find out the truth when we nail Kenton down.'

'And how do you propose to do that?'

'That's purely a matter of police routine,' Hargraves smiled, as he got to his feet. 'I'd like to thank you for being so frank about everything and helping us out. I'll keep you in touch with the final developments.'

Mason nodded and rose. 'Thanks a lot, inspector. The way it looks to me you're not going to have an easy job on your hands. However, best of luck!'

In another moment or two Mason had taken his departure. Hargraves returned slowly to his desk and sat down. He picked up a sandwich, bit into it, and then looked at Garson.

'Well, Garson, it means I've either got to use routine procedure to arrest Kenton, or else follow out whatever plan you may have in mind. Either way it's time we nabbed him.'

'I couldn't agree more — but routine procedure won't avail you much. You said you wanted absolute proof.'

'Certainly it would help things, but I don't think we dare delay much longer.

We've got a good deal of evidence on our side now. The bungalow in Notting Hill owned by Kenton. The gun all fixed up on the tripod. The taxi driver who took June Dawson to the bungalow . . . A host of things to incriminate Kenton if we decide to arrest him.'

'A host of things which a clever counsel might probably blow sky high,' Garson said, lighting a cigarette. 'On the other hand, if you feel like a further gamble there's another way.'

'For instance?'

'Kenton's at the Theater Royal for a short season. Right?'

'With somebody known as Maisie Grantham, his assistant. Yes, you're quite right.'

'I've made it my business to watch his performance at the Royal,' Garson said, surprisingly. 'Quite good it is, too. One part of his act calls for him to ask somebody to come up from the audience and be subjected to mental questions. All part of the act, of course.'

'Well?'

'Suppose,' Garson said, 'that June

Dawson was one of the people to go up from the audience?'

Hargraves stared. 'What! Good God, man, that would be the devil of a risk. Kenton would probably find some excuse for accidentally killing her. He wouldn't let a chance like that slip by, and you know it!'

'Sure I do, and that's why I suggested it. The point is: we must take precautions. It seems that Maisie Grantham is Kenton's only helper and we'd easily deal with her. Kenton himself does his work blindfolded, and in spite all the mumbo jumbo he talks about X-ray eyesight I'm willing to guarantee he can't see through his bandages — especially on a specially darkened stage, as it has to be for his act. My idea is to have June go up on that stage and announce who she is. After that, leave things to me.'

'I don't like it,' Hargraves muttered. 'I've already gambled once on that poor girl's life, and it was only because of you that she escaped being killed. If I tried it again and really misfired I'd be in the devil of a mess . . . and so would she.'

'I said I'd take care of things, man.'

'I heard you — but if anything happens to her blaming it on you won't be much help.'

'She *won't* be killed — don't worry. Look, here's how I've worked it out, and incidentally we'll need the help of a policewoman for this. Also we'll put in a bit of work with a tape recorder, since that's the instrument Jerome Kenton seems to love the most. A sort of 'hoist by his own petard' angle. As for the plan itself, listen to this . . . '

★   ★   ★

Right from the start, the present season at the Theater Royal had attracted big audiences, despite the competition of television — not particularly because of Jerome Kenton's startling mind-reading act, but because of the stellar names on the bill as a whole. And tonight was no exception.

The first house was emptying, and the second house entering when Garson, June Dawson, a hefty policewoman, and

Hargraves and Brice arrived at the theater in a taxi. The manager of the theater was already aware of their intended visit and had made special reservations for them in the front row of the orchestra stalls.

So the party entered with the normal patrons, Garson carrying a small case that contained a midget-sized transistor tape recorder. June, looking glamorous and yet somehow scared, which was hardly to be wondered at, was sandwiched between Garson and the policewoman, whilst Brice and Hargraves brought up the rear. Everything had been organized swiftly, in the typical Garson manner. It seemed hard for the inspector to realize that only that afternoon they had visited the sinister bungalow in Notting Hill Gate.

Quietly, the five took their places on the front row and there calmly sat, as any five in a party might sit when out for an evening's entertainment. What everybody else, except the staff and manager, did not know was that at all exits there unobtrusively stood constables, ready to be alerted at a moment's notice.

'Are you quite sure there's no danger to

anybody, Mr. Garson?' June asked anxiously, seated next to the scientist. 'I'm not so worried about myself, but if anybody else — '

'My dear young lady, you're worried about *yourself*, and nobody else — and you wouldn't be human if you weren't.' Garson glanced at her. Her face was pale beneath a delicate makeup and her eyes were frightened. Reassuringly he gripped her hand in a paternal fashion. 'There's nothing to worry about, June. Don't mind if I call you by your first name? I feel I've got to know you pretty well by now.'

'Of course I don't mind — and you're taking my mind off things by talking, aren't you?'

'Well, yes. Something like that . . . We've got this thing sewn up in a bag. Believe that! By the end of the evening Kenton will be safely in custody.'

June said no more, sensing that there was nothing to be gained by underlining how frightened she really was. In fact, had it not been for the quiet calm of the scientist beside her she would have run panicking out of the theater there and then. As it was she sat tight, her hands gripping the arm of her chair . . . Then in a moment or two the tension was broken somewhat as the orchestra struck up the overture, and presently the high-stepping chorus came into view.

So far, all was normal, and remained so through all the acts until the interval. Then Garson glanced at his program and gave Hargraves a warning look along the row. Hargraves nodded and sat back, apparently relaxed, but ready for anything.

'Kenton's next,' Garson murmured. 'Don't lose your nerve. I'll be at your side all the time.'

June nodded and tightened her lips. She gazed rigidly in front of her as the lights dimmed and the curtains swept back — to reveal a half lighted stage with one solitary figure garbed in black, standing impressively against a backdrop festooned with signs of the Zodiac.

'So *that's* him,' June whispered, as Garson's hand tightened on her arm. 'Just to look at him you wouldn't for a moment think that he — '

She paused as Jerome Kenton came slowly forward. At the center of the stage he stopped and stood surveying the audience with complete composure. Whatever murmuring there was slowly quieted and submerged into silence. The power of the man's personality was tremendous. Then at last he spoke.

'My friends, I do not know why Nature singled me out to have special gifts, and yet I have them. Strange powers! The power to read minds, the power to see through walls, the power to read the future.'

'A pity you don't read your own,' Garson murmured.

Impressive pause. Kenton's heavy bass voice and his obvious theatrical training were being used to full effect, and during the brief interval June studied the man with fascinated interest. Against the black clothing he wore his face was dead-white, whilst the cold, pitiless eyes stared into a solitary limelight which was now isolating him from the darkness around him.

'Tonight, my friends,' he continued, 'we are going to delve deep into the mysteries of the mind. We are going to explore, mentally, the reaches of space and time . . . But first, allow me to introduce the little lady who is invaluable to me in my performances — '

He moved his arm in a sweeping gesture, and from the wings came a slim, blonde woman. Her age was uncertain, but she still had a good deal of youth about her features and movements. In complete silence she came to Kenton's side.

'First,' Kenton said, 'I will prove to you that thoughts are not always so private as one would imagine — and for this experiment I shall require one or two volunteers to step up onto the stage. Of one thing I must warn you. Don't think about anything which you do not wish anybody else to know!'

There was a momentary laughter, rather uneasy it seemed, and then a moment of waiting as Kenton motioned with his hands for somebody to step forward. Then Garson got to his feet, his small case still in his hand. He nodded to June and she too rose — and then

Hargraves. The distance from the stage was too great for their features to be clearly recognized, especially with the auditorium in semi-gloom.

'Splendid!' Kenton exclaimed, bowing to them as they moved along towards the steps at the side of the stage. 'I assure you this is all in good fun.'

He clapped his hands sharply, and in response Maisie Grantham picked up a heavy pad and placed it over his eyes. Then followed a thick silk scarf that was tied over the pad and fastened at the back of the head ... By which time Garson, June, and Hargraves had arrived on the dimly lighted stage. The spotlight had now expired.

'Thank you, my friends, for your co-operation.' Kenton took an unhesitating step towards them, as though he could see quite well through his bandages, and gripped Garson's free hand tightly.

'Most kind of you, to volunteer, sir ... And the name, please?'

'George Smith, of London.'

'How are you, Mr. Smith? My assistant

will take care of you.'

Garson found himself handed over to the blonde and he remained by her side. Then Kenton seemed to think of something. He raised a hand slightly, in an unnecessarily dramatic gesture.

'But there is a lady amongst you. Is it not good manners to greet the lady first?'

'She's a trifle shy,' Hargraves explained. 'Anyway — I'm Geoffrey Gordon, and the young lady is right behind me.'

'I understand. How are you, Mr. Gordon — and thank you for coming up. My assistant will look after you — Ah, here we have the young lady. And such a delightful one, too! The name is — ?'

'June Dawson,' June said, in a firm, clear voice.

For a second Kenton seemed to hesitate. He moved a step nearer the girl.

'I'm sorry, but I didn't quite catch — '

'June Dawson.'

'June Dawson? I thank you.' Kenton had control of himself again. Hargraves stood watching intently, and so for that matter did Garson. Both men were aware of something. If Kenton could see through his blindfold, as he claimed, he ought to have no difficulty in recognizing June. On the other hand, if he could not — which was far more likely — there existed the possibility that, to him, this girl was a stranger and yet by coincidence having an identical name.

Whatever the case, Kenton went on talking, or rather intoning. He placed his hands on June's shoulders and held her firmly. She waited, quite sure that Kenton must have been aware of the fact that she was trembling violently.

'I shall now absorb your thoughts,' he said deliberately. 'Let there be perfect silence whilst I do so. Lights! Down with the lights, please!'

The spotlight faded from his face. What vague illumination there was gradually died. There were only faint reflections from the lights far backstage, and the glow from the exits and music stands of the orchestra. Garson moved a trifle so that he was right beside Maisie Grantham.

'Get into the wings,' he whispered in her ear.

She gave a start and glanced. 'But I

can't do that! I've got to help the boss to — '

'Do as you're told, miss,' Hargraves interrupted, low-voiced. 'You may get hurt if you don't. We're police officers.'

'Police officers! Oh, that's different.'

In the dim light the girl's face was astonished, but she began to move just the same. As she reached the wings two constables came momentarily into view, seized her arms, and pulled her out of sight.

Kenton, obviously unaware of the disappearance of his assistant, went on intoning steadily, calling on mystical — and probably mythical — gods to help him, and generally conveying the impression of throwing himself into a trance. When at last he took his hands from June's shoulders, Garson made a quick signal. Instantly June fled into the wings, leaving Garson and Hargraves watching narrowly. The audience, a little puzzled by these strange manoeuvers, began to stir restively.

'Quiet!' Kenton commanded abruptly. 'I feel the impact of strong mental disturbances. Please, I beg of you — absolute silence!'

The audience became still again, but they were not by any means satisfied with the proceedings — unless, of course, the comings and goings were all part of the act.

'June Dawson, be seated!' Kenton commanded; then he stood with his arms folded on his breast whilst Garson shifted a chair slightly to convey the impression of somebody sitting upon it.

'Now,' Kenton continued, 'I shall reveal what is in your mind. There is a sense of disturbance, as though you are afraid of something.'

Garson's foot reached out and poised itself ready over a remote control switch. With one hand he caught up a coil of slack wire.

'Why you are afraid I don't know,' Kenton continued. 'However, to facts: You are the daughter of a famous surgeon who died just recently, and there has been a great deal of trouble in your family. There will probably be more yet. Your future, in my estimation, is not a particularly happy one, and this I greatly regret. Your health will prove your biggest handicap in the days to come. That much I read . . . Now, as is my custom, I am open to answer any question you may ask.'

'Now for it,' Garson murmured to Hargraves. 'I knew he'd say that if he followed the same routine of other performances . . . ' He broke off and made a quick signal towards the wings.

'I said,' Kenton repeated, 'that I am willing to answer any question you may wish to ask — be it about yourself, your family, or any future event.'

Silently, in accordance with Hargraves' previous arrangement with the manager, the curtain came down. Kenton was not aware of the fact, though he did perhaps wonder at the curious blanketing effect that had come upon his voice. Beyond the curtains the hall lights came up and the manager said only a few words to explain the situation.

'Keep your seats, ladies and gentlemen. There is no need for alarm. A technical hitch has arisen which it will take a short time to straighten out. For various reasons we cannot ask the orchestra to play during this pause, so will you kindly bear with us . . . Thank you.'

On the stage the manager's voice did not penetrate — chiefly because of the thickness of the curtains, and also because he had spoken from a position on the front row of the Circle, again, by police arrangement. The audience seemed satisfied enough with his explanation for they settled down to wait.

'Come, come!' Kenton exclaimed, with a touch of impatience. 'Ask your questions, Miss Dawson. I have only a limited time at my disposal, and don't forget there are two gentlemen to follow you.'

'This is my first question,' came the voice of June Dawson, level and steady. 'For what reason did you decide to kill my brother Gerald?'

For a moment Kenton hesitated; then he made an irritated movement.

'I expect your questions to be serious, Miss Dawson! Please keep them so!'

'Why did you kill my sister Trudy? Why did you kill my father? Why did you try so hard to kill *me*, and yet failed to do so?'

Garson glanced towards the small tape recorder in the wings and gave Hargraves a significant look. The tape recorder, remote controlled by Garson's foot switch, was on a small table under a solitary light.

Kenton remained perfectly still as the new questions were directed at him. His hands did not move from their position on his breast. When he spoke, it was with complete control.

'Obviously, Miss Dawson, you are asking these absurd questions in the hope of confusing me — which fact you will readily understand, ladies and gentlemen,' he added, turning towards the curtained proscenium. 'I regret this happening, but at times one does get — '

'You killed my brother Gerald by making his car crash on the south coast road. You fixed a powerful spotlight on a tripod, and connected the lamp to the battery of your car. The dazzling light in the darkness blinded him for a moment and his car crashed . . . You warned him first on the 'phone that he was going to die. That was done by a tape recorder of the transistor variety. Later, somehow, you hypnotized him — '

Kenton swung, whipping something from his black robe. He fired a revolver point blank at the direction of the voice, the bandage still over his eyes. The tape recorder splintered under the impact of a bullet.

'Lights!' Garson shouted, and dived after Kenton as he hurtled towards the opposite wings, tearing off his bandages as he went. He did not get far. The waiting constables, duly placed at the stage exits, moved in and seized him. Furious, dishevelled, he glared at Hargraves and Garson as they came hurrying towards him.

'Journey's end, Kenton,' Hargraves said briefly. 'You've quite a bit of explaining to do . . . All right, boys, take him out.'

'What the devil are you doing?' Kenton demanded. 'You've nothing on me! Just because a lot of fool questions were asked by — '

'Those questions were right to the point,' Garson stated calmly. 'They were devised to produce the effect we intended — You deliberately fired at your imagined questioner to silence her, and you did it before witnesses which is just the way we wanted it. Fortunately, only a tape recorder has been damaged. That can be replaced, whereas a life can not.'

Struggling furiously, Kenton was hauled away down the brick walled corridor; then Hargraves glanced behind him as June came into view. Behind her came the policewoman in charge of Maisie Grantham — and behind them again appeared Sergeant Brice.

'Let's go;' Garson said briefly. 'The good people will want to get on with their entertainment, and we've done all we need here. I'll pick up the remains of my recorder later.'

*   *   *

It was towards midnight. June Dawson had been escorted safely home and now Garson, Hargraves, and Brice were all seated in the inspector's office, finishing off sandwiches and cups of tea from the canteen. Garson was looking particularly pleased with himself as he rubbed a hand through his ginger hair.

'Nice bit of strategy with that tape recorder — and as it happened it worked,' he commented. 'Just as we'd hoped, Kenton lost his grip on things and betrayed himself by pulling a gun on his imagined questioner. I suppose he thought he'd silence the evidence, even though he must have known at the back of his mind that he'd reached the end of his rope. It paid him back in his own coin, did that! He used a tape recorder for warnings: and we used June's tape-recorded voice to trap him . . . Anyway, let's have this would-be Svengali in here and see what he has to say for himself.'

Hargraves nodded and turned to the intercom. He switched on and gave a brief order.

'Bring Kenton in here, please.'

After a moment or two Kenton appeared, divested now of his stage trappings and attired in a normal suit. He seemed to have recovered his composure.

The only indication of his mood lay in the snaky glitter of his pale eyes. Hargraves felt the disturbing power of them as they gazed towards him, but he maintained his air of authority.

'Sit down!' he snapped, and then nodded to the constable to depart.

'Well, what now?' Kenton asked cynically, seating himself. 'Is this a reception committee?'

'You are entitled to make a statement,' Hargraves said. 'And I have to issue the usual caution that anything you may say will be taken down and may be used in evidence against you.'

Kenton shrugged. 'That's easy to deal with, then. I'm not saying anything.'

'Then maybe you can answer a few questions instead,' Garson put in. 'If you don't answer them we'll draw our own conclusions. I'm not a police officer so there are no restrictions on what I may ask. Right! We'll take Gerald Dawson first. How you killed him has already been explained to you. We're taking it that we are right in our assumptions.'

Silence. Kenton's eyes smoldered as he sat in his chair.

'Where,' asked Brice, going to the rear of Kenton, 'did you see Gerald Dawson in order to hypnotize him?'

'Don't waste your time,' Kenton sneered. 'A police officer has not the right to third-degree his prisoner — at least not in this country. As for your question, I'm not answering it. You're not frightening me, any of you . . . ' The cold, vindictive eyes flashed from one to the other. Garson and Hargraves sat undisturbed, their own gaze never flinching.

'Well, it doesn't really matter whether you answer the sergeant's question or not,' Garson commented. 'And don't get the idea we're trying anything suggestive of a third-degree. We're not. We're holding an informal conversation . . . You see, your girl friend Maisie Grantham has already told us the facts. She said you hypnotized Gerald in the lounge of the Cocktail Bar in Jerymn Street — '

'What! She couldn't have told you! I never said a word about going to — ' Kenton stopped, his lips tight.

'About going to the Cocktail Bar?' Hargraves suggested dryly. 'Never mind: you've told us all we wanted to know. We didn't know that *was* the place, but tracing Gerald Dawson's movements on the day of his death we know he went to the Cocktail Bar, the only place likely for you to make contact. Naturally you must have kept a close watch on him. The Bar's chief steward remembered a man of about your height, with pale eyes, being present . . . Most distinctive eyes you have, Kenton. Unfortunately for you!'

'Oh, shut up,' Kenton growled.

'Now, where are we? We have the problem of Gerald's murder solved. Presumably you were not at the theater on the particular night of the murder . . . Now to Trudy, the next in line. That doesn't present much of a problem. You obtained hyosycamus poison — probably from Dr. Mason, whom you hypnotized to give you the poison — then at a convenient moment at the Warlock party you got a previously computed quantity into Trudy's drink, calculating that it would take until about nine the following evening before it would have a fatal effect. Your calculations were quite good, or else you had a lot of luck, since Trudy died almost to the hour. Anything to say?'

Kenton said nothing and remained expressionless.

'Thirdly, Sir Robert,' Hargraves went on relentlessly. 'We do not know how you issued the post-hypnotic order for him to wire up his bath in order to produce fatal results — in which hypnotic order there would doubtless be instructions as to what to do in the matter of wiring and so forth — but it is a reasonable assumption that you followed him to the restaurant where he invariably lunched and, there — as in the manner of June Dawson — you placed him mentally under your command. He did exactly as ordered, even to taking his bath at the hour you had planted in his mind. The diabolical plan worked because you had not directly ordered him to kill himself — which naturally he would not have done . . . It may interest you to know, Kenton, that you are unique among criminals in that you use more mental than physical power to gain your ends . . . However, it's a gift that is not going to avail you much from now on.'

Kenton inspected his fingernails and hardly seemed aware that Hargraves was talking.

'Finally, June,' Hargraves said. 'It seems more than obvious that you invented a bogus reporter from the *Argus*, disguising yourself with a blond wig and contact lenses. In that role you used the same old formula of hypnotizing June, commanding her to make certain modifications to the television set after you had departed — and a further order telling her to switch the set on at nine o'clock. All this happened, but fortunately Mr. Garson here guessed the trick and saved her life — *and* he found out what had been done to the television. That must have shaken you quite a deal.'

Kenton seemed as though he were about to say something, then he apparently thought better of it. Hargraves eyed him narrowly before he continued:

'When you discovered you had failed to kill June you tried again — this time using

305

a bungalow of yours as the rendezvous. You hypnotized June in a restaurant and, true to orders, she went to the bungalow in question. Yet again she was saved — though the timely intervention of Mr. Garson. That was when we got on to you, Kenton, and forced your hand — at the theater tonight.'

'Very clever of you,' Kenton sneered, breaking his silence at last.

'Your whole scheme was quite ingeniously thought out,' Garson commented. 'I must allow you that. But you made the mistake of being over-elaborate. If you'd eliminated the 'phone calls we'd probably have been up a gum tree. However, you didn't, which made things come unstuck for you ... The warnings by tape-recorded voice — which voice was drawn and never actually existed — served to make your victims have the jitters, which added fuel to your hypnotic orders. Your remote control of the tape-recorder, your smuggling the recorder away in the guise of an old woman when things were getting a bit warm for you — Yes, all very ingenious. The only thing we lacked was an actual act of murder, and we got that at the theater. Now we possess that you haven't a leg to stand on.'

'You have to prove motive yet,' Kenton said grimly. 'And believe me my counsel won't be asleep when it comes to defending me.'

Hargraves gave a grim smile. 'We have the motive, Kenton. We know all about your past life — some of which you told to Sergeant Brice and myself when we called upon you. I'm referring to the death of your wife in a knife-throwing accident. The surgeon who tried to save her — and failed — was Sir Robert Dawson. You held a grudge against him, which finally became an obsession. Because he failed to save your wife you became embittered and decided that he and his loved ones should die — and to this end you devoted yourself with unholy thoroughness.

'You watched every move they made and when you knew their habits you chose your times. You also called into play a good deal of scientific experience. Primarily, I think, you were trying to

307

convey the impression that a murderer didn't really exist. You could be somewhere else — at the theater perhaps — when the fatalities occurred, and you imagined that that kind of alibi was absolutely foolproof. You were not even on the telephone when the warning voice spoke . . . All very clever, Kenton, as Mr. Garson has said, but not quite clever enough.'

'We'll see,' Kenton said sourly. 'And if I'm permitted to ask a question — what about Maisie Grantham? She knows nothing, so why did you arrest her? Last I saw of her that policewoman had her in tow.'

'All we did was question her, and we're quite satisfied that she's innocent. She has now gone home . . . But it will be a long time before you'll go home, Kenton — if at all.' Hargraves looked up. 'All right, sergeant, take him back where he belongs.'

As the office door closed Garson stretched his arms languidly.

'Well, Hargraves, that's that. If I may be allowed a quotation — 'Oh, what a tangled web we weave, when first we practice to deceive . . . ' Well, I'll be getting along. What do you think will happen to that blighter?'

'I couldn't care less. Probably detention during Her Majesty's pleasure — though it's at times like this I wonder if we should bring back the death sentence. But it makes no difference. Either way, society will be a darned sight sweeter without him!'

THE END

We do hope that you have enjoyed reading this large print book.

Did you know that all of our titles are available for purchase?

We publish a wide range of high quality large print books including:
Romances, Mysteries, Classics
General Fiction
Non Fiction and Westerns

Special interest titles available in large print are:
The Little Oxford Dictionary
Music Book, Song Book
Hymn Book, Service Book

Also available from us courtesy of Oxford University Press:
Young Readers' Dictionary
(large print edition)
Young Readers' Thesaurus
(large print edition)

For further information or a free brochure, please contact us at:
Ulverscroft Large Print Books Ltd.,
The Green, Bradgate Road, Anstey,
Leicester, LE7 7FU, England.
Tel: (00 44) **0116 236 4325**
Fax: (00 44) **0116 234 0205**

Other titles in the
Linford Mystery Library:

MURDER IN DUPLICATE

Peter Conway

When Jennifer Prentice, a student nurse, was found dead in a locked bathroom, Inspector Newton went to St. Aldhelm's Hospital to investigate . . . Newton finds the Matron, Miss Diana Digby Scott, unapproachable. Why was Alison Carter so disliked by Jennifer? Is Vernon Pritchard, the surgeon who was having an affair with Jennifer, telling the truth? Before Newton finds any answers, there is another death and he faces mortal danger himself.

A QUESTION OF MURDER

R. H. Lees

When Arthur Burnett died in the Rhodesian bush, Randall realised that Burnett was the one mentioned in the cryptogram. Inspector Sturman ridiculed Randall's suggestion that it could be foul play. So Randall proves that one of Burnett's African employees had been murdered and finds a mystic hill which only one African would dare to climb ... Whilst observing animal behaviour, he comes upon a gruesome scene and almost loses his own life before solving the mystery.

MURDER IN BURGOS

Lorette Foley

On holiday in Spain, Moss Coen is mistakenly arrested. He tries to escape from police custody, but in the city of Burgos, birthplace of El Cid, evidence connects him with murder. Unable to converse in Spanish, he then encounters Isabel Hervada Arias who has her reasons for offering help . . . There are other victims, and Moss finds himself a target for the killer whose ruthless ambition has led to more than one kind of crime.

UNWANTED WITNESS

George Douglas

Edmund Bradley, archivist at the University of Deniston is found murdered in his office. His expected visitor cannot be found, nor can Dr. Lewis Peel, with whom Bradley had quarrelled. Investigating, Hallam and Spratt confront missing 'top secret' papers and a second murder. The scene shifts to London, to a nursing home and a cremation at Golders Green. The mystery is unravelled when a crippled student determines to overcome his handicap by engaging in a forbidden climb of the university clock tower.